VIGILANTE MIDLIFE WOLF

MARKED OVER FORTY

MEG RIPLEY

SHIFTER NATION

CONTENTS

VIGILANTE MIDLIFE WOLF

Chapter 1	3
Chapter 2	16
Chapter 3	27
Chapter 4	36
Chapter 5	52
Chapter 6	71
Chapter 7	84
Chapter 8	99
Chapter 9	112
Chapter 10	123
Chapter 11	138
Chapter 12	151
Chapter 13	164
Chapter 14	178
Chapter 15	192
Chapter 16	206
Chapter 17	216
Epilogue	233
Hayden	247
Also by Meg Ripley	259

VIGILANTE MIDLIFE WOLF

1

"Easy there, Sherlock," Stephanie crooned to the hound at the end of her leash. The dog was constantly watching the trees on either side of them, his eyes wide and his ears perked in case something jumped out. He calmed only slightly at her words. "You're all right. That's a good boy."

"I'm surprised it's taking him this long to get used to the leash work," her daughter Annie commented, "especially with all these other dogs around to let him know it's okay."

Stephanie smiled down at the dog, who'd paused and turned his cocoa eyes to her, asking if he was still a good boy and doing everything right. The poor thing needed so much reassurance, and she was happy to give it to him. It was a shame no one had been willing to do so in the first place. "He'll get it. He's been through some rough times, and it takes some rescues longer than others to be convinced that nothing bad will happen to them again. We don't even know the extent of what Sherlock has been through."

Annie nodded. "Being stuck in that cage overgrown with weeds had to be bad enough."

"I can't argue with that." Stephanie frowned, easily remembering when she'd been called out to the foreclosed home. The mortgage holder had already tried animal control, but the officer was busy. Somehow, Dr. Stephanie Caldwell had been next on the list. It wasn't the kind of thing she normally did, but her intuition had told her to go. She'd found Sherlock hunkered in the back corner of an outdoor pen, barely visible through the thick weeds that'd grown inside it over the summer. The only reason anyone had even known a dog was present was by its mournful howls. "Out there howling like the hound of the Baskervilles. I doubt he was ever out on a leash during that time. Or if he was, only bad things happened."

Her daughter let out a long sigh.

"What's the matter?"

Annie stooped to pick a burr off Jacques, the

little chihuahua she was walking. Penelope, the pit bull mix, took great interest and nosed her hand. She smiled and scratched her between the ears. "It's just that I've been doubting the whole vet school thing."

Stephanie raised an eyebrow. "How come?"

"Well, dogs like these, for instance. They needed help and homes. Now, they have good vet care, plenty of healthy food, and reliable shelter. I'm happy to see they're taken care of, but I know there will always be more."

"Veterinary work isn't necessarily rescue work," Stephanie pointed out. "I know the two are often intertwined, and I've certainly allowed that to happen in my practice, but you have the privilege of choosing what to do with your career. You can move to Beverly Hills and do nothing but give acupuncture to celebrity dogs if you'd like."

Annie wrinkled her nose. "Yeah right, Mom. You know I'd never do that."

No, she probably wouldn't. Annie had always been the kind of kid who'd rather roll in the mud than put on makeup, and that hadn't changed much as she'd gotten older. She was strong and practical and had always seemed to know what she wanted. That made it all the more surprising that she was questioning herself now. "My point is, you have to do what makes you happy. I've always been proud of you for choosing the veterinary path, but my concern has been that you don't do it just because you think you have to."

"I'm not. It's just always felt like this thing I need to do. Tons of animals out there need help in one way or another, and I want to be there for them. I'm just overwhelmed, I guess."

"It'll do that to you." Annie would be finishing her vet tech degree that year and moving on to veterinary school. That would be a lot, but it wouldn't be the end of it. Stephanie had spent so many days with sick pets, gone to bed completely exhausted, and then dragged herself back up the next day. It was once she'd combined traditional medicine with naturopathic therapies that things had started to feel better for her, more relaxed. It was the path she was destined to find, and Annie would need to find hers, too. "Keep your head up, kiddo. You're smart, and you've been doing great in school. Whatever you decide to do, you'll be awesome at it."

Annie gave her a small smile. "Yeah, that's what Dad said, too. We went out to lunch yesterday, and—whoa! What has gotten into you guys? Easy, easy!" She tightened her grip on the two leashes in her hand. Little Jacques didn't take much to restrain, but Penelope had pulled her leash to the end and was straining against her harness.

Sherlock was freaking out in his own way. His nose was in the air, and his tail stood straight. Instead of trying to run forward, he was backing up, trying to get away from whatever it was that had spooked him so much. Stephanie put her hand on his back and took a deep breath, trying to tap into his feelings. "He's really scared. Do you see anything up ahead?"

"Here." Brave as ever, Annie handed over her two leashes and moved forward.

They'd gone walking in those woods dozens of times, if not more. The most they'd ever encountered were squirrels and other hikers. Stephanie knew she had no real reason to worry, but for once, she questioned her daughter's grit. With three trembling dogs, she waited.

"Um, Mom?"

"Yeah?"

Annie reappeared from around the bend. "You're not going to believe this because I'm not sure I do, but there's a wolf up here."

"What?" A tremor of energy shot through Stephanie. She loved wolves, and though they were in the area, encountering one was rare. She'd always seen a particular one come around back when she was in college, but it must've grown used to people.

"I'm not sure it's alive, though," Annie explained, looking over her shoulder. "I'm going to see if it has a heartbeat."

"Be careful!" The mother in her could override anything else, including the veterinarian and animal lover. This was her daughter; if anything happened to her, she'd never forgive herself. Inside, she was now just as edgy as the dogs.

Annie returned a moment later, shaking her head. "I think it's a goner."

"Let me have a look." Putting the dogs in her daughter's care, Stephanie headed forward. Her hiking boots were solid against the firm ground, and she felt a cool breeze toying with the strands of hair that'd come loose from her long braid. It pushed her forward on the trail, towards what she couldn't be entirely sure.

The wolf lay on the side of the path, its jaw slack and eyes closed. It certainly didn't look like it had any life left in it, but she had to be sure. Slowly, carefully, Stephanie approached. She murmured to the creature as she did so, making it aware of her, even if only on a subconscious level.

Kneeling, she pressed her hand gently to the animal's chest.

She felt nothing.

Worry jolted through her, and she slid her hand up until it rested just inside the wolf's armpit, right where its front leg met its body. She closed her eyes and focused, tuning out the chirping birds and the rustling leaves. There. It was slight, but she could feel it. Stephanie thought she sensed something else, perhaps a mental message somehow making its way through despite the wolf's pitiful state.

Stephanie opened her eyes and pulled back. She could see no visible injuries on the wolf, but perhaps they were internal. She had two options, and she already knew which one she would take as she returned to Annie. "It's alive, but barely. I'm taking it to the office. Let's go put the dogs in the cab of the truck, and we'll load him in the back."

Annie turned immediately back toward the parking lot. Sherlock was more than happy to head back in that direction, even if Jacques and Penelope were much more interested in what lay ahead of them on the path. "Shouldn't we call animal control or something?"

That had been the other option, one Stephanie had quickly ruled out. "There's only so much they can do, and they're often backed up as it is. By the time someone gets out here, he might be gone." Reaching the truck, Stephanie pulled a small tarp out of the back while Annie loaded the dogs into the cab. She couldn't remember exactly why she had it back there with her other supplies, but she was glad she did.

"Holy shit," Annie whispered with excitement a few minutes later as they carefully grabbed the wolf's paws and slid him onto a tarp. "This is incredible!"

Stephanie smiled to herself. Annie might occasionally doubt her future as a vet, but Stephanie never would. That thrill would keep her going, and she'd find more of them.

The wolf was heavy as they carried it out to the truck. She knew they shouldn't be doing this. They should probably do exactly as Annie had suggested and call the proper authorities. But something inside her argued quickly against the notion. She had to do something. There was a reason they'd happened to come out there on the same day the wolf had. Her heart thundered in her throat as they carefully slid the tarp into the bed of the truck and she closed the back of the camper shell.

The drive to the office felt much longer than it

actually was, as Stephanie took care not to brake or accelerate too hard.

"Mom?"

"Hm?" Stephanie frowned as she took a curve in the road that led them back into town, hoping they didn't encounter too many stoplights.

"Let's say this wolf is all right, that you're able to fix whatever's wrong with him."

"That's the idea," Stephanie replied.

"Well, then what? I mean, you can't just have a wolf running around your office. It might be dangerous."

Yes. A wolf certainly should be considered dangerous, especially one cornered in an exam room. If he'd been healthy and on his feet when they'd found him out in the woods, he would've likely just run away. He couldn't exactly do that, though, and Stephanie had caught sight of those gleaming white teeth. "I'll figure it out. He's certainly no threat right now."

Stephanie backed up to the rear entrance of the building. Hoping no one was watching them, she unlocked the back door, and the two women carried the wolf inside on the tarp. "Let's put him in exam room five. It's the biggest one."

The table in there had been specially ordered to

accommodate bigger dogs, but she never expected to use it for a wolf. He made even the oversized table look small by comparison.

"What do you need me to do?"

Stephanie could hear the dogs barking from the truck. "Go ahead and take those guys back to your place. It's probably best if you just keep them tonight. I'm going to get started here. I'll call you if I need anything."

Annie hesitated in the exam room doorway. "Are you sure?"

Looking at the beast, there were a lot of things Stephanie didn't know. She didn't know what had possessed her to bring a wild animal into her clinic, even if it was closed for the day. She didn't know what she'd do with him if she could save his life, nor did she know exactly how she'd get him back out to the woods. All she knew was that she had to try. "Yeah. I'm sure."

Once alone, Stephanie easily fell back into her training and moved through the process one step at a time. With the luxury of a stethoscope this time, she checked his heart rate and other vitals. He definitely wasn't doing well, but she had yet to find a cause. A quick x-ray didn't reveal much, except for some old wounds that'd healed long ago. She pulled a couple vials of blood to be run through the lab. With every step, she watched for any signs that he might regain consciousness. Though hope thrilled in her that he might, it tangled with fear.

She laid her hand on his fur, feeling the density of it. It was so thick that it practically pushed back against the palm of her hand. Stephanie once again dared to close her eyes as she sought a link with the animal's thoughts. She'd known for quite some time that she could reach animals on a psychic level, and she let her mind seek out a connection. It'd always been easier with some animals than others, but she found something right away: flashes of fear and pain. Underneath was something else, something strong that she couldn't identify. She hadn't felt anything like it in a long time.

"Something's blocked in you," she whispered as she moved over to the drawers on the side of the room. "I don't know what it is. I'll be honest. I'm not even entirely sure of what will help, but we're going to give this a try. It's worked for lots of sick cats and dogs. People, too, though I can't help but think animals are more open to it since no one has told them otherwise."

Moving around to the other side of the table, she knew she could give the wolf a stimulant to increase his heart rate and try to wake him, but it would likely cause him pain or make him agitated. Acupuncture was the best route, and it was one she was confident in. With expert ease and care, she parted the thick fur and inserted the tiny needles. They would open the wolf's meridians and restore the flow of qi, encouraging his body to heal itself.

It took far less time than she'd imagined. His paw twitched, then his muzzle, showing off those incredibly sharp teeth. The fur along his back rippled as the muscles beneath spasmed.

Stephanie took her stethoscope off her neck and checked his heart rate. Not only was it back, but it was thrumming quickly. "What's going on with you?" she whispered.

The wolf's body exploded with movement. His legs jerked and stretched, lengthening before her very eyes. His fur sank into his skin, leaving only a head of dark hair. A soft crack sounded through the room as the wolf's muzzle shrank and squeezed, its tail disappearing at the same time.

Stephanie leapt back. She hit a cart of supplies, sending numerous items clattering to the floor. Something glass broke, but she didn't look for it. She pressed back further until she ran into the wall of the exam room and had no other place to go. Her mind refused to understand what she was seeing. It was a nightmare. Horror rippled beneath her skin as she watched the wolf transform into a man.

No, not just any man. Terrified, she took in the dark hair over the strong brows. The square jaw and the wide shoulders. A rush of attraction funneled through her chest despite her panic as the nightmare became more and more real.

She recognized him. She *knew* him. One moment, she'd had a wolf on the exam table. Now, somehow, in some way that extended past the far reaches of her imagination, it was Bennett Westbrook, her high school sweetheart.

2

BENNETT PUSHED AGAINST THE SLICK STAINLESS STEEL surface beneath him, shoving himself upright. The metal was cold against his skin, and the lights were too bright. The whole place smelled like a weird combination of antiseptic and essential oils. That horrible screeching noise wasn't making things any better. Bennett shook his head and tried to get his bearings.

He finally figured out where that awful noise was coming from. In the corner of the small room, as far away from him as possible, a woman stood with her shoulders hunched against the drywall. She stared at him, keeping her wide eyes on him as her hands patted the nearby countertop, searching for something.

A few things started to click together in his addled brain. The last place he remembered being was in the forest. Things had been bad, and then it'd all gone dark. Now, judging by the weird table he was on and the poster on the wall that lectured about the dangers of heartworms, he was in a veterinarian's office. It made zero sense, but at least he was putting reality together around him.

The woman was the biggest problem. She'd stopped screaming now, but her breath was heaving in her chest. Her long hair was bundled into a frazzled braid that fell down over her shoulder, and her green eyes glittered with fear. There were fine lines on either side of them now, and he spotted a few threads of gray in that braid. Even so, it was impossible not to recognize the face he knew so well from high school, the face he'd dreamed of at night. It was Stephanie Caldwell, the only woman he'd ever loved.

"You...you...you changed," she stammered. Stephanie's hand landed on a tray of tools, and she snatched one up. She glared at the useless tongue depressor in her hand and tossed it aside.

Bennett had to smile. "Hey, I'm not gonna say the years have been kind to me, but everyone looks different after a few decades."

"No!" she snarled. Stephanie straightened up a bit against the wall. Her eyes ran over every part of his body. "You were a wolf. Like two seconds ago, you were a friggin' wolf! And then you changed into... you!"

Shit. So much for keeping the shifter secret. In all of his forty-seven years, he'd never revealed himself to anyone but fellow shifters, and he wouldn't have done it now, either. Bennett was getting some of his bearings, but that didn't mean the world around him made any sense. "What am I doing here?"

"What the hell is going on?" she asked at the same time.

"Why are you here?" he tried.

"How did you do that?" Both of their questions echoed through the room simultaneously.

Bennett sighed. This was bizarre as hell, but he wasn't the one who'd just seen an animal turn into a man. As far as he was concerned, that meant the burden of making sense of this for both of them was on him. "I have plenty of questions I'd like to ask you, but we'll start with what you just saw."

Stephanie gave him a very firm blink and nodded. "That would be good. I hope it means I haven't lost my mind."

"You haven't." He bent forward and rubbed his hands up and down his face. How the hell was he supposed to explain this? It was simple enough, but only because he'd been living it. His wolf was surging inside him, demanding answers. It was also demanding that he get closer to Stephanie. Given her current state, he knew it wasn't a good idea. Either way, battling with his beast wasn't making this any easier. "I'm a shifter. I spend most of my time looking the way you see me right now, but I was born with the ability to change into a wolf."

"So you've always been able to do this?" She was still studying him, her eyes following the line of his shoulder, ears, and nose.

His stomach dropped with guilt. "Yeah."

"Even back in high school?"

She didn't say 'when we were dating,' but he knew that had to be what she truly wanted to know. "Yes. I'm sorry I didn't tell you before, but I couldn't. It's not the sort of thing we can just announce. It might freak someone out." Bennett offered her another smile.

Stephanie let out a syllable somewhere between a laugh and a grunt. "That's a pretty fair bet. I still don't understand, though. Why are you like this? You said you were born this way?"

He nodded. "Just like the rest of my family."

"There are *more*?" Stephanie pushed herself away from the wall now. She found a wheeled stool amidst the wreckage of medical supplies and dog treats she'd scattered on the floor and sat down. "This is a lot to absorb."

"It's a lot to tell," he replied honestly. "Think about what it'd be like if you tried to explain to someone what it was like being human."

"I don't think I'd even know where to start," she admitted. "I'm still not sure I haven't gone off the deep end. One minute, my daughter and I were carrying a nearly dead wolf out of the woods, and the next, the wolf turned into you. You can tell me all day long that there are shifters in the world, but my mind is just refusing to understand."

He pressed his lips together. That was exactly why they didn't tell anyone. Plenty of other creatures were in fiction and movies, but humans could handle that because they *knew* they weren't real. Bennett and his family—as well as plenty of other people in Eugene and even all over the world—were completely made up as far as most humans were concerned.

But at least she'd started answering his questions, whether she realized it or not. "So you brought me here? Is there anyone else here with us?"

"Yes. No." Stephanie took a deep breath and let it out. "I mean, my daughter and I found the wolf—you—while we were out for a short hike. You were in bad shape, so we brought you back here to my office. I sent her home with the dogs, and the office is closed for the day. We're alone."

That should've been reassuring, but it only sent a stab of desire through his body. Even after all these years, she was still just as beautiful as ever. In fact, if he squinted a little, he might've thought she looked exactly the same as she did the last time he'd seen her. Maybe a little curvier, but he sure didn't mind that.

Stay on track.

Okay, so there weren't any other witnesses to his shift. Good. "Did anyone else see you when you were in the woods? When you found me? Or did you call anyone to report this?"

Stephanie shook her head. "No. It's a cool day, and we didn't see anyone else on the trail. I didn't call animal control because I knew they'd never get to you in time. You were dying. I had to do something, and it needed to be quick. I figured I'd practice medicine first and then answer for it later."

"Thank you, and I think animal control would be grateful, too. They wouldn't appreciate finding me in a cage. Actually, that's something else I don't understand. You found me when I was still in my wolf form. I never would've voluntarily shifted in front of you, Stephanie. I wouldn't have put you or myself through that." This was a big part of what'd been bothering him ever since he'd woken up. Bennett knew he'd been injured, but it took energy to shift. He definitely hadn't had it, and this whole scenario never should've happened.

"You said this is something you have control over?" She was going back and forth between putting her head in her hands in complete despair and staring at him like he was the most fascinating thing she'd seen. Right now, it was the latter.

He might be offended if that look was coming from anyone else, but he knew how much she loved science. Stephanie was the girl in all the advanced placement classes, the one who won all the science fairs, the one who voluntarily spent her free time doing research and learning new things. It was a passion that he'd always admired. "Usually, yes. Once I learned how."

"So your parents had to teach you? I'm sorry." She swallowed as she continued to stare at him. "It's just…kind of fascinating once you get past the scary parts."

Seeing the hint of a smile on her face made him relax a bit, but Bennett knew he couldn't relax for long. If he had to let his secret out in front of anyone, he was glad it was Stephanie. She was a human, but she was probably one of very few he could trust, if any. The secret was becoming less of a problem to him now. He was more concerned with the consequences of how he'd gotten there. If anyone had seen her pull him from the woods, they'd have a much bigger situation on their hands.

"Listen, Stephanie." He had to figure out how to explain the rest of this. Bennett swept his hand down the back of his neck. His palm brushed something, and a tingling sensation moved through him. Reaching back, he plucked a tiny gold needle out of his skin. "What the hell is this?"

"Oh." She shot to her feet and moved around behind him. Stephanie's hand grazed against his skin as she carefully plucked several more out of him and dropped them in the sharps bin. "They're acupuncture needles. I was trying to figure out what was wrong with you. The traditional methods weren't getting me anywhere, and I sensed that your qi was blocked. I tried these."

A shiver moved down his spine, but it wasn't because of the needles. They'd never been more than a few feet away from each other over the last few minutes, but this close proximity was difficult to bear. Still holding the one needle in his hand, Bennett turned to her. "Just what kind of vet's office do you run, anyway?"

"An integrative one," she explained simply. "I use traditional methods when they're called for, but there are a lot of other techniques out there that get ignored by vets. I think they fill the gaps in rather nicely, and acupuncture is one of them."

"Interesting." He twirled the little needle in his fingers. "When did you do this?"

She thought for a second, and her brows shot up. "Right before you shifted, actually. Do you think that had something to do with it?"

"I'm not completely sure. I may look like a human on the outside, but not much is known about shifters in terms of medicine." They could ponder the implications all night, but Bennett forced himself back on track again. There were always certain priorities in a shifter's life, and right now, he had to be sure he took care of one of them. In fact, he had a hell of a lot he needed to tell her, and this whole experience had been disoriented enough that he wasn't sure he'd ever get it all out. "I need you to do me a favor."

"What's that?" She'd relaxed a bit when they'd spoken of acupuncture, but he could sense her getting tense again.

He moved closer, reaching out and taking her wrist. Her pulse thumped unsteadily under his fingers. Bennett felt his body electrifying. "You can't tell anyone about who I really am. It's a secret that my family and many families like us have been keeping under wraps for a long time and with good reason."

Stephanie's eyes searched his face. Was she looking for the wolf again? "I see why. But what about my daughter? How am I going to explain this to her?"

"You're not," Bennett replied quickly. Now that Stephanie was no longer screaming or waving tongue depressors at him, he hopped down from the exam table. He'd only held off before because he hadn't wanted to scare her any more than he already had. "Think about how you reacted; you're a woman of science and logic. And you even knew who I was. The impact would be catastrophic for everyone like me, and it probably wouldn't go over well with the general human population, either."

"No." Stephanie looked down at his hand where it gripped her wrist. "It wouldn't."

"I know we didn't leave off on the best of terms the last time we saw each other." In fact, the pain of that day had come flooding back to him the moment he'd realized it was her. He'd hurt her, but he'd had no choice. "Please, just promise me that you won't tell anyone. I need to know that my secret is safe with you."

3

STEPHANIE LOOKED UP INTO THOSE FAMILIAR DARK eyes. She couldn't believe what she'd just seen. A creature she'd been absolutely certain was a wolf had transformed right in front of her. He'd become a man she hadn't seen in over twenty years, one she'd never expected to see again. Now, he was standing there in her office, asking for her help.

He'd meant so much to her back when she was a teenager. They'd been young, and so many friends and family members had spoken of young love as something that was sweet but would never last. That hadn't stopped Stephanie from believing it was much more. She'd had a sense of certainty that they belonged together, and her conviction had been so strong that she'd barely been able to handle it when he'd shattered her dreams about a future together.

She'd put that pain aside for a long time, but it stabbed through her heart anew as he stood there and asked her to keep his secret.

"This is, um, really wild." Stephanie turned toward the exam room door. She could tell him to get the hell out of her office. She could go to the news or whoever else and explain what she'd just seen. There was a chance that someone would believe her and she'd get money or fame for outing these shifters, or there was a chance she'd be tossed in the looney bin. The thing was, she found she didn't want to tell anyone at all. Bennett might have broken her heart, but that didn't mean she could do that to him.

"I know." His voice was desperate behind her. "I'm really sorry all of this has happened the way it has. If it helps at all, I was tempted to tell you many times. This isn't how I would've done it, though."

Stephanie let out a long sigh. "I feel like there's a lot I don't know about you, but I do believe you on that. It's kind of funny, isn't it? That I would happen to be the one to find you? I mean, it could've happened to anyone, right?"

When she turned back to him, his eyes looked

darker than before. "Right," he replied in a near-whisper.

She got the feeling there was something else he wasn't telling her. Hell, there was probably a shit ton he wasn't telling her. How could he even begin when he wasn't human? "Don't worry about it, Bennett. I'm not going to say anything. No one would believe me, anyway." Stephanie meant that last part to be light-hearted, but the truth of the statement prevented that.

"I should probably get going. I've caused enough trouble for you." He moved toward the exam room door.

"I'll give you a ride home. My truck is out back. You'll just have to excuse the dog hair." The words were out of her mouth before she'd really even thought about them, but she didn't correct herself. Was she just trying to find a way to spend more time with him? That was crazy. Granted, he was still just as hot as he'd ever been back then. Stephanie hadn't been the only one to notice his striking good looks, and several girls had done anything they could to try to undermine their relationship. Not everyone aged well after high school, but Bennett was definitely the exception. No longer as wiry as he'd been, he'd filled out with wide shoulders and a chest that you could lay your head on for hours. His square jaw was strong, almost enough to make him look a bit too cocky, but then those soft dark eyes let you know he was far more than just muscle.

She bit her lip and forced herself back in line as she led the way out of the exam room, down the short hall, and into the office where she'd left her keys.

"You own this place?" he asked.

"Mmhm. I was an associate for some other local vets for a while, but once I found my niche, I knew I needed to head out on my own. My methods don't exactly fit in with what everyone else wants to do."

Bennett glanced around, absorbing the fridge of raw dog food in the lobby next to the display of essential oils. "Given all those little needles in the back of my neck, I'd say you're right. This is a nice place, though. You must not be doing too badly."

"We get by." Stephanie felt a bit of pride as they worked their way toward the back of the building, with each exam room opening on either side of them and the lab and tech room toward the end. "It took a long time to get to this point. I was limping along with used equipment or borrowing from others, and it was tough to keep the books balanced.

I'm happy with where it is now, and I'm doubly happy that Annie works here with me."

"Your daughter, right?"

"Right. She's in college, and she's my vet tech. She's incredible. I love seeing her passion, and it blooms anew every now and then. It's amazing." Stephanie leaned into the lab and flicked off the light. She'd left it on in her haste to figure out what was wrong with the wolf, but the wolf wasn't really a problem anymore. "What about you? What do you do for a living these days?"

They'd reached the back door, and she'd turned around to face him. Bennett narrowed his eyes, and his jaw hardened. "I'm self-employed."

"Ah." She smiled, but it faded as she saw that he wasn't going to elaborate. Stephanie knew what that usually meant, and she wouldn't push the issue. So, he was in between jobs. Why embarrass him? Hell, did shifters even have the same kinds of jobs as humans? Every time she asked a question, the answer only made more questions arise.

"Hold these for a second." She stepped outside and handed him her keys. "This back door will lock itself, but it's always a pain in the ass to close. It takes both hands. And a shoulder." She pulled in hard on the latch, ensuring it wouldn't catch on the frame, then shoved the door shut. It was a tight fit, which made it so difficult, but there was definitely no getting it back open without a key once it was secure.

"Get in the truck."

"What?" Stephanie turned around to see Bennett standing there with his fists curled at his sides. His shoulders were tight as he stared at the tree line that the parking lot backed up to.

Stephanie's heart did a jumping jack as she took in the three dark shapes that emerged from the shadows and into the dim remainder of light, padding forward soundlessly. She'd never even have noticed them if it hadn't been for Bennett. Their heads were low and their hackles raised. Their eyes were focused solely on Bennett and Stephanie.

Images flashed in her mind of wolves tearing each other apart, blood dripping down their chins as they snarled and looked for their next victim. Anger and vicious contempt rippled through her, and Stephanie knew without a doubt that she was now part of the equation. "I take it they aren't friends of yours."

"I'm not strong enough to fight them right now. Not all three." He spoke quietly and kept his focus on the newcomers.

Stephanie took an automatic step backward but

immediately realized what a bad situation this was. She'd have to turn her back on the wolves in order to get the damn door open. They could cover the bit of asphalt between them in no time, and all that blood wouldn't just be part of a psychic vision. "Oh, god."

"Truck. *Now*. I'm driving." Bennett was off like a shot.

"What?" Stephanie went after him. She'd parked close to the door so she and Annie could get the wolf inside without any issue. With these beasts bearing down on her, she might as well have been running a marathon. This was definitely a race she hadn't trained for, either.

Bennett hurried around to the driver's side, but the passenger's side was right there. She reached out, her hand moving as slowly as a nightmare. They were coming. She could hear their paws now, their nails scratching slightly on the asphalt. Deep growls emanated from their throats. Her body was moving, but it wasn't enough. Her visions became stronger. They weren't just ripping other wolves apart. They were tearing her limbs from her body. Bile rose in her throat as she flung open the door and shoved herself up into the seat. Stephanie slammed the door behind her just as one of the wolves reached it, his teeth clanging against the old metal.

The engine roared to life. Stephanie felt the definitive thump of the front bumper grazing one of the wolves as they pealed out onto the side street.

"You might want to put your seatbelt on," Bennett advised as he slammed his foot on the accelerator.

"What the hell is going on?" She was dizzy and off-balance, barely able to believe what she'd just seen. It'd been terrifying enough to have a wolf in her office, and then doubly scary for him to turn into a man. Actually having the beasts come after her, though, was just too much to bear. "Why did they do that?"

His head swiveled as he checked traffic before flying through a red light, leaving several cars honking in his wake.

"Shit!"

"Sorry." He showed absolutely no sign of slowing down. Bennett maneuvered the big truck like it was a sports car, flinging it around corners and zipping through stop signs as they threaded through several neighborhoods.

Stephanie cringed every time she heard her equipment sliding around in the back. At least it was under the camper shell and wouldn't be going anywhere. She risked a glance backward through the rear windshield. It was all so typical and suburban. "It's not like they could really follow us, right?"

"Are you already forgetting they're not just regular wolves?" Bennett challenged. "They could very easily have a vehicle stashed nearby."

Stephanie clung to the safety strap as they rounded another corner. "But they're shifters, right? Like you? Why would they be after you?"

"It's just not that simple."

4

"I'm sorry, Stephanie."

"For what? Driving my truck like there's no such thing as an insurance deductible?" she snapped.

She'd always been a bit sassy. Bennett had always liked that about her, and now he was finding he still did. "Hey, this old thing handles pretty well, actually."

"I guess if we're still alive, that's something."

Bennett made another quick right and then watched the rearview. No one was behind them now, and he hadn't seen any sign that they were being followed. They'd gotten away for now, but that had been far too close of a call. If Stephanie didn't like his driving, she really wasn't going to like what he had to say next.

"We're alive," he agreed, "for the moment. But our lives are still in danger."

She was watching the mirrors just as vigilantly as he was, but she snapped her head around to look at him. "Why, though? I know you've already had to explain some pretty major things, like your existence, but you're going to have to lay this all out for me, Bennett. I'm not sure how much more I can take."

"Well, that's what I was apologizing for." He readjusted his grip on the wheel and worked his way toward the edge of town. "They've seen you with me, and that means you're associated with me. You have to come with me to my place."

"No." She shook her head and dug her nails into the upholstery. "I just want to go home. If you need the truck to get to wherever you're going, fine, but drop me off first. I'll give you the address."

"I can't do that, Stephanie." He pulled out onto the highway and accelerated smoothly. "Just because we didn't see them follow us doesn't mean they aren't aware of our location. If we go to your place, they'll know exactly where you live. You'd be taken out in no time. My place is secure enough that they'll never get to you."

"But who are they?" she demanded, her pitch

rising as tears glimmered in her eyes. "I've got to know what's going on, Bennett. I'm a logical, rational person, and I'm desperately hoping that a good explanation will help it all make sense. And maybe I won't feel like I'm living in a horror movie."

Bennett could pretty much guarantee that wouldn't be the outcome, but she did deserve an explanation. "Okay, first of all, not all shifters are on good terms with each other. It's not like all humans are friends, so I think that's pretty easy to understand. Right?"

She swallowed. "Right."

"We have different factions. They're usually based at least loosely around a family unit, and we call them packs." He was moving slowly through this, feeling like he was trudging through mud. He didn't want to get to the part she really had to know now, though.

"Just like a wolf pack," she affirmed, still obviously trying to get a hold of herself.

"Some of them get along. Some of them even have alliances. Other times, we're nothing but enemies. Those guys you just saw back there are part of the Silvergrove pack. More specifically, they're the Bloodmoon Crew. Basically, they're a group within the Silvergroves who are running a crime organization."

She stared at him for a long moment, her head bobbing slightly with the movement of the truck. "Shifters...*and* the mob?"

"Basically." Bennett ran his hand across his chin, hating himself for the whole thing. He'd never meant to get anyone else involved. His line of work meant he operated alone, and there was good reason for it. Most people couldn't handle this. Stephanie looked like she might evaporate if he turned the heater up too high, so she clearly wasn't handling it at all. "They might be shifters, but they're just like any other crime organization you've ever heard of. They want to gain power, and they'll do it by whatever means necessary. It doesn't matter who or what stands in their way."

"Holy shit." She sank into her seat, rested her elbow on the door, and tented her hand over her eyes. "Here I was thinking this was just a normal day. I just went out for a walk with Annie and the dogs. Simple enough. Now I'm in trouble with the werewolf mob. Fantastic."

Bennett was acutely aware that it wasn't just the mob part that was making her upset. He'd dealt her one hell of a blow by revealing himself as a shifter, and there'd been no choice but to explain the truth about that. It was a hell of a lot to lay on her, especially in one day. "I was hired to take the Bloodmoon Crew down."

"Which explains why there are bitemarks in my truck and fur in my grill," she retorted. Her brows knotted together and she sat up straight. "Wait. Wait, wait, wait."

"What?" Bennett kept his foot pressed firmly on the accelerator. Whatever reservations she had wouldn't stop him from getting as far away from the Bloodmoon Crew as he could.

"You were *hired* to take them down?" She was staring at him hard now, her eyes boring into his cheek.

"That's right." His job wasn't an easy one to explain, but he rarely ever found himself in a position of having to do so. "My first attempt didn't go very well. It turns out they're much stronger than they were the last time I ran into them, but that was personal."

He kept his gaze hard on the road as they flew along the highway, the dark shadows of the trees thickening on either side of them. Bennett had first come to know the Bloodmoon Crew a long time ago, and he'd been more than eager for this chance to get the revenge he craved. He'd underestimated them, though.

Bennett was living in the past, but Stephanie was still very much in the present moment. "So what are you? Some sort of vigilante or something?"

"It's not exactly how I refer to myself, but the job descriptions line up." He knew how it sounded, and she'd certainly gotten a good sense of how his life looked. He wasn't just some innocent kid with a secret, not anymore. He had a lot of secrets, and most of them weren't the kind anyone liked to hear. Bennett swore he felt her pulling back from him, and the wolf inside him howled in protest. He'd finally found his mate again. Sure, Bennett had known she was around somewhere, but he'd stopped looking a long time ago. Then fate had tossed them back together, and it was hard not to think there was a good reason for it.

"I thought vigilantes were only in movies," she muttered.

"Kind of like people who turn into wolves?" he asked.

"Yeah." Her smile was sad, and she once again looked on the verge of tears. "Just like that."

For a minute or so, the only sounds were from the engine and the tires on the road. "You said your first attempt at taking down these guys didn't go well. Is that what happened to you in the woods? Because I didn't really find much evidence of injury, not enough to make you so close to death. And then, when we were behind the office and those three appeared, you said you weren't strong enough to fight them. It doesn't make sense to me. Not that I would expect anyone to fight three wolves," she added quickly. "Or even one."

They were getting close to the turn-off, and Bennett slowed down. "Shifters heal quickly when we're in our animal forms. I'm not saying it works perfectly, and it's not like we can't die, but we're definitely not the same as humans. By the time you found me, my physical wounds had probably mostly healed. I know just how much blood I'd left behind, though. That part takes a bit longer. If I'd chosen to fight them, I would've been risking your life just as much as mine. More, really. What are you doing?"

She pulled her breath in through her nose and held it. After several seconds, she let it out slowly through slightly pursed lips. Stephanie's eyes were closed, and she'd placed her hands palms down on her lap. "Breathing."

"Aren't we all?"

Stephanie opened her eyes and gave him a sideways glance. "For the moment, and it sounds like we're lucky to have that. I'm just trying to calm myself the hell down, okay?"

"Right." He slowed down and turned. The place where the trees split and the old dirt road took over was almost impossible to see. There were no reflectors or markers, which was just the way he wanted it. People flew past there all the time and had no clue it was there. Or if they did see it, they assumed it was one of the many old logging roads in the area. It wound through the trees and up to a gate.

Not being in his vehicle, he didn't have the remote that would allow him to open the gate without getting out. "I'll be right back."

He got out and listened, letting his wolf guide him. The moon was bright that night, Selene's blessing illuminating the woods. There were no threats, not tonight. As he stepped into the truck's headlights to undo the latch, Bennett knew he was the only threat at the moment. He'd done a hell of a number on Stephanie. He'd put quite a heavy load on her mind, and he couldn't blame her in the least for freaking out. She'd just learned about a whole world around her that she hadn't known about. It was a lot to put on anyone, and it made him feel like a real asshole. Whether or not Stephanie thought so, he'd find out eventually.

"Did I see a security camera blinking on top of that fence post?" she asked when he climbed back in the driver's seat.

At least her natural curiosity had once again overwhelmed her fear. Bennett had already seen that happen back at her clinic when her knowledge of his shifter secret was both fear and fascination. In a lot of ways, she hadn't changed. "One of them, yes. I let that one be seen as a warning, but it's just the beginning of what I've got here."

Once he'd pulled through and shut the gate behind them, he continued. "I have cameras all over this property, even mounted on the trees where they can monitor the trails in the woods. It's all synced up with my cell phone, so I know what's happening. There are also tripwires and a few nasty surprises for anyone who tries to come anywhere near the house without my permission."

"A little much, if you ask me," she murmured as she ducked down to get a better look at everything through the windshield.

"It has to be with my line of work. I do what I'm hired to do, just like anyone else. Sometimes, my targets get wind of what's happening before I get the chance to complete the gig, though, or someone else wants revenge. It's not exactly glamorous." Bennett pulled up in front of the garage, where he'd left his own vehicle when he'd gone out in search of the Bloodmoon Crew in wolf form. He shut off the engine and handed the keys back to Stephanie.

"Your driving has improved over the years, but not by much," she grumbled, though she was smiling.

"What do you mean?" He kept his head up and his ears alert as he brought her up the walkway and unlocked the gate. If Bennett had been driving his own vehicle, he would've come in through the garage. That felt inherently safer. Despite all the precautionary measures he'd taken to keep his property as secure as possible, he still felt exposed.

She laughed lightly, though her raw nerves could still be heard on the edge. "I still remember when you borrowed Tommy McFadden's old muscle car and picked me up in it. I thought I was going to die that night."

"Only of sheer amazement for just how badass it was, right?" He held the gate open to let her through before he came through himself and shut it behind him, ensuring it was locked. "I remember that night well. I thought for sure I'd impress you. It's funny what boys think will impress girls at that age."

She laughed again, a sound he liked way too much. "The same can be said for us girls, you know. I clearly remember thinking that if I just had a new color of nail polish or the right pair of earrings, it would make all the difference. I don't think you ever noticed."

"Sure I did," Bennett countered.

"You did not."

"Yes, I did. You painted your nails with little watermelon slices that one time. I was surprised because it didn't seem like the kind of thing you'd ever do. You were just more practical than that. Not that I didn't like the watermelons, though."

Stephanie turned to him and held out her hands, wiggling her fingers to show off her bare nails. "I guess I've gone back to my practical ways."

Bennett might've noticed her nail polish back then, but right now, he was focused on the fact there weren't any rings on her fingers. He hadn't even thought to ask if she was married. That was stupid of him, considering she had a daughter, but Stephanie had yet to mention a husband. His wolf churned within him once again, happy to be this close to her after all these years. The damn beast had never cared about what was practical.

They reached the porch steps, and Stephanie pointed to the sign nailed to the railing. "Beware of Dog? Let me guess: Rottweiler? Pitbull? German shepherd?"

"Well, he's the primary force in all the defenses I've set up here." Bennett crossed the porch and punched in his security code. "I should've warned you about him before. In fact, I'll probably have to introduce the two of you slowly so he doesn't try to attack you for coming onto his territory."

He opened the door. The little Pomeranian came charging through the living room in a fluff ball of fury. He jumped up on his hind legs to give an excited yap of greeting to Bennett. He nearly tripped over the threshold as he tried to get to Stephanie, his poofy tail waggling and his tiny tongue lolling out the side of his mouth.

"Easy there, Rambo." Bennett held the door open until they were all safely inside the house, with the dog still hopping excitedly around Stephanie's ankles.

"Oh, my goodness! Just look at you!" She held out her hand for Rambo to sniff, and as soon as she knew he'd accepted her, she was petting him all over.

"You must be an ancient little man. Oh, yes. That's the spot, isn't it? You're just the best boy, aren't you?"

"He is," Bennett agreed, finally feeling more relaxed now that he knew they were both safely inside his personal fortress. "Most people come to a new house and look at the flooring or the architecture. You plop yourself right on the floor and make friends with the dog. Not that I really expected anything different."

"I couldn't possibly just ignore this little guy. Could I? Definitely not. Well, all right then. You just make yourself right at home." This last part was her response when the dog marched up to her lap and settled himself in her arms.

"I think he found himself another sucker," Bennett said when she stood, still cradling the funny little dog in her arms. "He found me, and I sure as hell couldn't resist him."

"Did you get him from a senior shelter or something?" She was still rubbing his gray muzzle and digging her fingers down into his fluffy fur.

"From a crime scene, actually." He grinned when her brows shot up. "I used to be on the police force. His owner had been killed. Since there weren't any family members stepping up to take him, he was destined for the pound. I just couldn't let it happen."

He reached out and scratched Rambo's ear, but the dog was completely taken with Stephanie.

"He's very grateful," she said with a smile.

"I should hope so, considering how much I pay for his special senior dog food. Speaking of, come in the kitchen. I think we could both use some dinner."

"Isn't there something we should be doing?" she asked as she followed him.

Bennett opened the fridge. "Like what?"

"I don't know. I guess it just feels strange to run away from three people who were trying to kill us and then just go have dinner." She perched on a bar stool, still holding Rambo.

"You have to eat, even when the chips are down." He pulled several containers out and set them on the counter. "I learned that a long time ago. You can't think straight when you're hungry."

"I guess that's true. Is there anything I can do to help?"

He didn't want to ask for any help at all. Not from her. Not when he'd completely changed her life in the span of an hour. "You can feed Rambo if you want. That bin right over there has his food in it. He gets one scoop, and don't let him con you out of any more. His twiggy little legs won't hold him up if he gets any fatter."

"Come here, baby," she crooned as she brought the dog over to his bowl and set him down gently. "All right, now you've given me a moment to look at the flooring and the architecture."

"And?" He'd always just picked things he liked. It wasn't like anyone else really ever saw the place. It was different with her, though.

"And I'm guessing your vigilante work—or whatever you'd prefer to call it—must pay the bills just fine." She crossed to the sink and washed her hands.

"The dirty work always pays the best because no one else wants to do it." He gave her a bowl of shredded lettuce and offered the numerous toppings. "I'll let you put on whatever you'd like."

Stephanie looked over the offerings of chicken, black beans, guacamole, and tomatoes. "You like to eat healthy?"

"Not always, but I figured you did." With his bowl in hand, he led the way to the table.

"How long have you been doing this, anyway?" Stephanie stirred the contents of her bowl, making sure the guac was evenly spread over everything. "Unless you're sick of having to explain every little thing to me."

"No, that's fine." Looking at her across the table, Bennett knew what he felt inside. It'd never really left. He'd just been able to shove it down. That was no longer possible now that she was right there, and he'd explain any detail she wanted as long as it meant she was still right there, right within arm's reach.

Damn, it felt good to have her in his home.

5

SHE SHOULDN'T BE THIS COMFORTABLE AROUND HIM. He'd taken everything she'd ever learned in school and turned it on its head. Then he'd taken the safe and secure lifestyle she thought she was leading and completely reversed that as well. She'd been absolutely terrified, as anyone in their right mind would be once they'd found out someone was trying to kill them. As soon as she'd worked on her breathing techniques, though, she'd known that Bennett himself wasn't the problem.

Or, at least, not *that* kind of problem.

Being around him felt too damn good. It shouldn't, considering everything else. But just as she'd noticed back at her clinic, something inside her felt differently. It made her feel safe. Comfortable. Stephanie found herself studying the lines of his hands or the way his eyes crinkled at the corners when he smiled. It didn't hurt that she'd felt the warm happiness Rambo had exuded as soon as he'd realized his person was home. Stephanie knew the best way to judge someone was by the way animals acted around them, and Rambo had certainly given Bennett his stamp of approval.

They were little things, but they all added up. She should be figuring out how she was going to get herself out of this situation instead of sitting down to eat and chatting about their work histories.

"I've been doing this for several years now. It's not the kind of thing you get anniversary plaques for." He quirked his mouth into an ironic grin as he stabbed his fork through his salad. "Like I said before, I was on the police force. I did well, and I was promoted to detective. The problem with that is sometimes the people higher up on the chain don't want you to actually do your job."

"What do you mean?" Stephanie could easily see him as a police officer. He'd always been the kid who wanted to fight for what was right, standing up against bullies in school and making sure that others didn't get picked on. It didn't even matter if he knew the other kids. He just saw a situation and always seemed to know how to handle it.

"The key word of organized crime is 'organized.' They have everything all laid out, and they follow a plan. That makes it easy for the right person to pick up on because there are patterns if you're paying attention. But that organization also means they've taken care of anyone who might stand in their way, including police chiefs." His brows drew down as he spoke.

The nervousness that Stephanie had felt before came roiling back into her stomach. It was terrifying to know someone wanted to kill you, even more so to know no one might be able to help.

"I knew it had to be the Bloodmoon Crew, even before I had any true evidence against them. I went to my chief, presented my case, and told him what I wanted to do. That was my job, right? That was what I was supposed to do. But he blew me off, told me it wasn't worth the department's time, and that I was making up drama where there wasn't any. It didn't take long to figure out that he was in cahoots with them."

"That's horrible," Stephanie protested.

"Yeah, well, life is kind of horrible sometimes." His eyes lasered onto hers for a minute before drifting back down to his bowl. "You're right. A person in a position of power like that shouldn't be capable of being bought, but it happens. It probably happens more than we like to imagine. I wouldn't let it stand in my way, so I started my investigation regardless. I did it on my own time, and I didn't let it interfere with the official police work I was doing, but they have their ways. The chief found out about it, and I was fired. Rightly so, since I was going against a direct order."

"But you had a good reason to." Stephanie didn't know why she was trying to justify this for him. He didn't need that from her, but she wanted to understand. Somehow, it seemed as though understanding might make it all right.

Bennett shrugged. "I had more reason than most people would realize, but the force doesn't exactly want you to open up a case based on your own personal desire for revenge."

The salad was delicious, but food didn't appeal to her much at the moment. Still, Stephanie forced herself to eat. She knew he was right and that she would need the fuel later. "You mentioned you had some sort of vendetta against them." She'd still been trying to wrap her head around all this when he'd said something before. She still was, really, but it was getting easier to understand as she acquired more information.

"Yeah." Bennett looked over just as Rambo finished his dinner and turned to him. He got up and let the little puff ball outside. "Do you remember that restaurant my dad used to run?"

"Definitely." She smiled at the memory. "Your dad always had student specials for all the broke high school kids so they could still eat there. I was pretty sure he made some of them up on the spot just because he wanted to feed us. And you looked pretty cute in that half-apron when you got stuck being a waiter. I remember hearing that it burned down."

"It did. All the papers said it was an accident, something with the electrical work. That's what the authorities told them, but it wasn't true. The Blood-moon Crew did it." He sat down heavily. "My sister was closing up, and she was inside. Rosa didn't make it."

Stephanie let out a breath of grief for him. She had no idea. She'd been so caught up in everything she'd had going on with college that she'd paid little attention to any local news back then.

"It was hard on all of us, of course, but my father took it the worst." Bennett threaded his fingers together and laid his hands on the table, his knuckles white. "He kept saying it was his fault. Mom and I figured he was just saying that because he was grieving, the obvious stuff. He had a heart attack two weeks later. I was able to get to the hospital as soon as they brought him in, and just before he died, he told me the truth."

Seeing him relive all this was hard, especially knowing it was for her sake. But Stephanie also knew she couldn't stop him now. He wouldn't tell her if he didn't want to. Every part of his body showed how much anger still lived in him over all of this. She couldn't do anything to make it better other than to listen.

"Nelson Silvergrove is the Alpha of the Silvergrove pack. That's essentially like the leader or father figure, though it carries a lot more weight than that for shifters. He's also the one heading up the Bloodmoon Crew. He and his goons had come in for a meal at Westbrook's. My father didn't like them, but he wouldn't bring shifter politics into his business. They were just there to eat like anyone else. When it came time to pay the bill, they told him they wouldn't. They said it was a small price for him to pay to keep his place open. Dad was a kind and generous man, but he didn't put up with anyone's bullshit. He told them they'd pay or get banned from the restaurant, simple as that, just like anyone else. Two days later, it was gone, along with Rosa. Dad held on for a couple of weeks, but that heart attack killed him. I lost half of my family in less than a month."

"Bennett, I—I hardly even know what to say except that I'm sorry." She rose from her seat, wishing she could put her arms around him and hold him. It wouldn't make things any better. In fact, her current involvement in his life had probably only made it more complicated. Stephanie went to the sink to rinse her bowl. "I'm so sorry you had to suffer a loss like that."

"It was bad," he admitted, his voice growing closer as he stood from the table, "but there was another loss before that, one that has affected me just as much. Maybe even more."

She turned to find that he was right behind her. Bennett's eyes were burning into hers, but they'd lost the intense laser focus they'd had while he was discussing his family and former career. They were soft now, a dark velvet that warmed her skin by several degrees. Stephanie reminded herself—definitely not for the first time—that they weren't just horny teenagers anymore, and she had to be mature about this, but it was impossible when he looked at her that way. It was a look of desire and adoration. It was a look that said more than that, but she wanted to hear it and know for sure. "What do you mean?"

"Stephanie." Her name was heavy on his lips. "I never wanted to break up with you all those years ago."

What had felt like pure desire a moment ago quickly turned into confusion. "Then why did you? You never really told me." She'd put that day out of her mind long ago, but that didn't mean she'd forgotten.

Stephanie had known something was off about Bennett. He'd been moody and distant. When she'd asked about it, he'd just said he hadn't been getting along with his parents. Everyone their age felt that way at the time, so she hadn't worried about it. The next thing she knew, he'd told her it was time for him to move on.

"I know. I couldn't." Bennett took another step and closed the gap between them. His hands grazed her hips and then closed slowly around them, his strong fingers pressing appreciatively against her curves. "It wasn't my decision, Stephanie. My parents made me do it. I know that sounds like I'm just putting the blame on them, but believe me, I never would've broken up with you."

Electricity bolted through her body. Bennett had always been able to light that inner spark for her, and it wasn't any different now. He was just close enough to her that his body brushed against hers slightly as they breathed, a tantalizing tease and a reminder of their past. "If you'd told me, maybe we would've figured it out."

"No." He reached up and brushed her braid behind her shoulder before resting his palm along her jawline. "Stephanie, they hadn't liked the idea of me being with a human. I couldn't tell you that without telling you everything."

"Wait." She pulled her face out of his grasp and stepped away from the sink, releasing herself from the spell he so easily cast over her. Stephanie kept herself at a safe distance, one where she might not find her brain so muddled by her lust for him. "I always had a feeling they weren't thrilled about me, but that's so unfair. It's not like being human is anything I can change."

"I'm not saying it was right." Bennett moved toward her, but he stopped short of getting as close as he'd been only a moment ago. "I shouldn't have done what they asked, but you know how it is when you're just a kid. They were my parents."

Stephanie shook her head. "I get that, Bennett. I really do. I'm not saying I blame you, not really. We're all just a product of where we come from. But it's a little hurtful."

"As it should be. No one should think that way, but people do. You see it happen all the time. The only difference between us is that no one would ever know just how different you and I are simply by looking at us from the outside." He moved forward again, his eyes tracing her face, searching.

"I know that." She really did. It was all perfectly logical and made sense. That was the sort of thing Stephanie usually liked, but it wasn't adding up for her right now.

"No one had ever made me feel the way you did." He took her hand now, rubbing his thumbs against the back of it. "The way you still do, actually. It'd been a long time, but it doesn't feel like anything has changed. I still want you, Stephanie. I always have."

A lot in her life had changed that day, considering everything she'd learned. The world was a much bigger and scarier place than she'd ever realized, but he was right. When it came down to their feelings, it was all the same. He still gave her that same rush of excitement every time she looked at him. Even when he'd freshly changed out of his wolf form, she'd still felt that same attraction. As things had calmed down and they'd had time to talk, she'd found herself falling easily into those old emotions.

"Bennett, I can't deny that the way we feel about each other hasn't changed. But some other things haven't changed, either. If my being human broke us up back then, what would make things any different now? I'm still a human, and you're still a shifter. Do you think your family is any more willing to accept that?" It was hard to talk rationally about such things when every part of her body was commanding her to take just one step forward. She wanted to throw all caution out the window and dive back in, but she couldn't. Not when she knew such a big issue was hanging over their heads.

Judging by the genuine smile on his face now, Bennett didn't see it that way. "The thing is, I'm forty-seven now. I don't really care what they think. My mother is the only close family I have left besides my pack. She and I haven't discussed this in a long time, but it isn't about what she wants. It's about what *I* want." Bennett reached out and grabbed her hip. He pulled her against him and then slid his hand around to the small of her back. "There's something else, too."

Her heartbeat was completely out of control, and it thundered through every part of her body. She felt it in her lips every time she looked at his mouth. When she saw the deep craving in his eyes, her blood heated as the answering sweetness echoed in her core. "What's that?" she dared to ask.

"Shifters believe we're destined to be with one special person. Our fated mates were separated from us before our souls inhabited these bodies, but we've retained a connection with them, a pull we can't deny. It's not the same as just being attracted to someone. It's much more than that. It's finding the other part of who you are. Stephanie, I always believed that was you. I just didn't know how to express it back then. I didn't even know how to be sure."

She shivered despite the heat that rampaged through her body. "And now?"

"Now I know. We were always supposed to be together. Life separated us for a while, but fate brought us back into each other's lives. I can feel it every time I look at you. My wolf lives inside me even when you see me looking like this, and it knows. It can't stand the idea of being without you. It wants to protect you and take care of you. It wants you, and so do I." He pressed a kiss against her lips, his mouth soft but demanding enough to let her know he truly meant every word.

Stephanie closed her eyes and fell into that kiss, her body melting in his arms. She was a woman of science. She liked and appreciated logic and reason. What Bennett had just told her defied all that, but damn it if it wasn't the most romantic thing she'd ever heard. She kissed him back, finding his mouth both new and familiar. As she did, Stephanie searched herself for any sign of that connection that Bennett had just spoken of. Was that it? That thread of unending yearning she'd always felt for him, that sometimes haunted her in her dreams or flashed through her mind at the most inappropriate moments? The one that she'd ignored all these years and that had come to life again? She wasn't sure, but she wanted to find out.

"I want you, too, Bennett. I don't know anything about fate, not in the way you're referring to it. I do know that I always thought we'd be together forever, no matter how ridiculous that sounded when we were so young. I also know that nothing else along the way has compared to you." Abandoning all the logic and reason that'd guided her through so much of her life, Stephanie kissed him again.

Bennett's strong arms closed around her upper legs and lifted her from the ground. What a thrill it'd been when he'd done that to her back in the day, making her feel weightless, and it was no less thrilling now. Stephanie yielded to the dizzying feeling of being carried down the hallways as she kissed him, her tongue roving over the soft surface of his.

Her arousal went to the very marrow of her bones as he kicked open a door at the end of the hall. He loosened his grip, slowly letting her slide to the floor. Stephanie noted the hard bulge at the front of his jeans, igniting an ache of need inside her.

Stephanie reached around behind him to find the hem of his t-shirt, a blaze of excitement firing through her trembling fingers every time they brushed against the heat of his skin. Lifting his shirt over his head and tossing it on a nearby chair, Stephanie took in the raw delight of his torso. A few angled lines of thin scars traced over his muscled chest. A dusting of dark hair was just the right amount to drive her wild as she ran her palms across his pecs and down his strong abs. It narrowed at his navel and disappeared into the waistband of his jeans, reminding her of what was yet to be discovered. As with everything else between them lately, this was the same person she'd always known, yet he'd grown into a whole new man. "Damn, the years have been good to you."

Bennett's warm hands glided down her arms. "I like to think there's more to me than just my chest."

"Oh, there is." She dragged her lips across his wide chest, leaving kisses in her wake. "Your abs, your arms, your lips."

He bent his head and plundered her mouth, pressing his lips hard against hers as his tongue stroked inside. His hands gripped her backside and held her firmly against him, reminding her once again of just what he had waiting for her.

Stephanie's breath had disappeared from her lungs by the time he pulled back, and she watched with dizzy pleasure as he pushed her flannel off her shoulders and twisted his hands in the material of her fitted tee. "You," he said as he pulled it off and revealed her bra. "You're the one who the years have been good to."

Dipping his head, Bennett pressed kisses down her throat and along her collarbone. He lingered at the curve of her shoulder, seeming to find pleasure in even the most mundane of places. He worked his lips down to the tops of her generous breasts as his hand slid around her back.

She knew exactly what he was doing, but she still felt a small shock as he easily unclasped her bra with one hand. "I see your skills are still sharp."

"You never know when they'll come in handy." Bennett flicked her bra to the side. He cradled her breasts in his warm hands and laved her nipple with his tongue before sucking it into the heat of his mouth.

Clinging to him, Stephanie tipped her head back and lost herself in the pure pleasure of his adorations. He still knew just how to touch her, even in as small of a gesture as running his hands over her hips. The only difference was that they knew what they were doing now and didn't have to sneak around in the back of a car. He held her with confidence and let her know his desires. Yes, all of this was far better after forty.

Bennett reluctantly pulled away from her breasts to unfasten the button of her jeans. He shimmied the denim down off her hips, once again kissing his way through his latest discovery. His lips burned against her stomach and dipped below her navel. He stripped her panties away, and a groan of appreciation rumbled in his throat.

Stephanie was just reaching for his fly when his arms wrapped around her and her feet left the ground. She bounced softly onto the mattress, laughing, and was pushing herself up onto her elbows when Bennett resumed his kisses once again. She surrendered, falling back onto the sheets as he gently pushed her knees apart. He kissed the inside of each thigh before going for his intended target. His mouth was hot, moving slowly at first as he found her sensitive pearl. Once he had her warmed up, though, his tongue and lips became far more demanding. Her legs trembled and her breath came in stuttered gasps. Her core tightened and twisted as he pushed her further, finding just the right spot and flicking the tip of his tongue against it. She was vaguely aware of him taking off the rest of his clothes in the process, but her mind wanted only to focus on what he could make her do.

She tipped over the edge, gasping and crying out, tortured by the sheer delight welling up inside her body. A brief chill tingled against her skin as Bennett pulled away before coming up onto the bed with her, easily sliding his hardness into her silky depths.

His manhood filled her, creating an all-new ecstasy within her as the echoes of her orgasm rippled against him. She'd hardly had a second to catch her breath, but as his hips moved against hers, she found that she didn't want to. Stephanie ran her hands down his back as she clung to him, reveling in the feeling of his skin against hers, his weight above her, and the way their bodies fit together so perfectly.

Bennett let out a heavy breath as his girth swelled inside her. Stephanie gripped him harder, wanting this for him but feeling that tight coil building again within herself as well. She cried out as they peaked, her body burning and her mind wild as they crossed into oblivion.

She laid with her head on his chest afterward, feeling her body relax in a way she was sure it hadn't in a long time. Man or wolf, fated or not, all she really knew was that it felt right.

Until an alarm blasted through the room.

Bennett pulled his shoulder out from underneath her and jumped out of bed. He searched for his pants and pulled out his phone. "I've got all the security cameras tied to this, and some of them are going off."

Her heartbeat quickened. That'd happened a lot that night, but now, it was out of fear. Had the Bloodmoon Crew found them? She clenched her teeth and waited, wondering what she ought to be doing.

Where would they go? How could she defend herself?

"Oh. It's just Rambo." He turned the phone to show her the little Pomeranian making his way out of the yard and back up onto the porch. "I let him out after dinner but then got a little distracted."

As Bennett threw on his pants and stepped out of the bedroom to fetch the dog, Stephanie tried to slow her racing mind and heart. It was just Rambo, and everything was fine. But how long would it remain that way? She and Bennett had found something remarkable between them, but they were still in danger.

6

BENNETT OPENED HIS EYES AND STUDIED THE SLEEPING form next to him. Her hair had come loose from its braid and was splayed out over the pillow. The sheets and blankets were pulled up just below her shoulders, leaving just enough skin to remind him that she was completely naked underneath. He rolled on his side and pulled her against him, kissing the back of her neck.

A pleased groan escaped her lips. "Well, good morning to you, too."

"It certainly is." In the back of his mind, he knew he wasn't in the clear. The Bloodmoon Crew was after him, who would be overjoyed to see him dead. For Bennett, though, that wasn't a whole lot different from everyday life. What he was much more excited about was having his mate there in his bed, looking sleepy and happy. A bit of the morning sunlight had managed to work its way in through the curtains, highlighting her body and awakening his desire once again. He pushed himself up on his elbow so he could trail his kisses across her shoulder while his hand explored the lovely softness of her belly and breasts. His arousal told him just what they ought to do with their morning.

Stephanie bolted upright.

"Sorry," Bennett mumbled. "I just figured—"

"No, it's not that." She reached over to the nightstand and looked at her phone. "I've got to get to work."

"That's not a good idea." Since she was already sliding out of bed, Bennett regretfully did the same. He quickly tugged on his underwear and pants. "Nelson's crew saw you with me at your office. They'll be looking for the next opportunity to ambush you."

Goosebumps stood out on her arms as she pulled on her jeans. Stephanie slowed down a bit as she buttoned them. "So what am I supposed to do?"

"Stay here with me." The words came so easily. "We're safe here. I need to work some things out, but it's best if we lay low for a while."

"I can't do that." Irritation crossed her face as she put on her bra.

He had to admit that even when she was in a rush, it was pretty sexy to see her adjust her breasts once she'd done up the clasp and pulled up the straps. It was distracting enough that Bennett lost his train of thought for a minute, and it was an important one to stay on. "Why not? It's your business. Can't you just take a sick day or something?"

"I've got clients, people who've been scheduled to come in for months. I can't just not be there. I know it sounds like I should be able to, but being self-employed doesn't mean I can just disappear whenever I want." She looked under the edge of the bed for her socks. "Besides, Annie will be coming in this morning. She's got all my dogs with her, too. How could I explain that to her? Hell, how am I going to explain any of this to her?"

It was a question he'd already heard her ask herself once, but he had no better answers than she did. "We'll think of something, but Stephanie, it's dangerous out there. You have no idea just how good these guys are. They've taken countless lives over the years, and they've injured or stolen from plenty of others along the way. They've never had to deal with the consequences of their actions, and they don't expect to. That makes them even more dangerous."

She gestured helplessly with her hands. "So come with me, then."

"What?" He'd opened a drawer to pull out a clean shirt, but he stared at her instead. Not that she was difficult to look at, moving around his bedroom with just a bra and jeans on. Yes, she'd definitely changed over the years, but they were definitely changes he could appreciate.

"Come with me to the office. I know it isn't a perfect idea, and you probably have other things you need to do, but—"

"No. I'll go. That'll work." His wolf wanted nothing more than to keep her safe and protected, and he latched onto the idea quickly. She was right. It definitely wasn't a perfect plan. He didn't feel he could guarantee her safety at her office the same way he could there, but it seemed to be the best solution at the moment.

"Shit." She'd picked up her t-shirt and flannel from the back of the armchair. "I'm forty-seven years old, and I'm about to make the walk of shame into my own clinic wearing the same shirt I wore yesterday."

Bennett pulled a black undershirt from the

drawer he'd just opened and handed it to her. "Try this. And this." He snagged a flannel from the closet.

Stephanie looked at the items doubtfully. She tugged on the undershirt and tucked it into her jeans. The ribbed material stretched across her breasts in a way that made him want to change his mind about going anywhere other than back to bed. The flannel was too big, but his wolf was more intrigued by the idea of her in his clothes than by style. "That should work."

"Well enough, I guess," she said with a laugh. "When I left the house yesterday, I should've planned for coming across my high school sweetheart and falling into bed with him."

"Is that how you think of me?"

"Of course." She'd sat down in the armchair to pull on her hiking boots but now glanced up at him. "Weren't we?"

"Yeah. We were. It's just nice to hear that. I'll go feed Rambo and make some breakfast." Bennett smiled as he headed out into the kitchen. Plenty of times, he'd figured Stephanie probably hated him for what he'd done to her, and he'd had no way to show her just how much he regretted it. She'd let him know with just a couple of words that he'd been wrong all along, and something healed inside him as he scooped up Rambo's breakfast.

That didn't change the fact that he wasn't entirely comfortable with their plan for the day. "I just want to make it very clear that you can't let your guard down for a second," Bennett said when they were back in her truck and taking the winding road out to the highway. "I don't think it's a good idea to give the Bloodmoon Crew even the slightest advantage."

"I understand, but what's my other option? To stop living my life? To hide in a hole forever, wondering if the danger has passed? I've got obligations to my clients, Bennett. There are sick pets who need me and owners who want the kind of treatment I give them. They can go get their rabies shots anywhere, but that's not the case with everything else I offer." She chewed her bottom lip.

"You always did do that when you were nervous." He reached over and put his hand on her thigh, rubbing his palm down her jeans. Bennett meant it as a comforting gesture, but it was just making his own pants tighter. "We'll make it work the best we can. It'll give us a chance to get to know each other all over again."

She put her hand on top of his. "I think you know me pretty well."

"Not everything. I'll even start off with something awkward." He waited a moment while she turned to him and nodded. "You have a daughter. Were you married?"

"I was, for a few years."

"Now, tell me: what kind of man would be stupid enough to leave a woman like you? Other than me, of course." He hadn't let himself think about it much yet. He and Stephanie had gone their separate ways years ago, and he had no right to be jealous of anyone she might end up with. In fact, he considered himself lucky that she was single right now. It was just hard to understand how.

"A gay one," she replied simply.

His eyes widened, and the truck wobbled toward the white line. "Oh."

Stephanie laughed. "As far as divorce stories go, ours is relatively boring other than that fact. Brian and I met in college. He was quiet and sweet, and we got along well. It was just sort of comfortable. I knew a lot of girls who were looking for some big, dramatic love story, but Brian and I were just sort of automatic. We got married after college, and we had Annie. He was a good father, but after a while, I

knew something was off between us. He came out of
the closet when Annie was about three."

"Was it a big fight?" It was none of his business,
not really. She was his mate, and he knew it with
every fiber of his being. He wanted to know every
detail of her life, the same way he wanted to memo-
rize every square inch of her body.

"No, not at all. I was shocked and devastated, but
we didn't fight about it." She smiled as she looked
out the window. "An uncontested divorce is pretty
cheap, too. I wasn't going to hold him back and keep
him from living the life he truly wanted just because
he hadn't figured this out by the time he'd said his
vows. I wanted him to be happy and wanted myself
to be, too. That never would've happened if we'd
continued living the way we'd been. He's been a
great father to Annie all along, and we're on friendly
terms. Compared to the situations I see a lot of
people in, it's pretty good."

"I'm glad it worked out for you, then. Have you
seen anyone else?"

"No, not really. I've had too many other things I
needed or wanted to do."

Bennett scanned the trees, realizing he hadn't
been as vigilant as he should be. He was getting to

know Stephanie all over again. It was so strange, but it was a feeling he was more than happy to deal with.

He carefully backed into the same parking spot where her truck had been the previous day. "Are you sure about this?" he asked when he saw her hands shaking as she took out her keys.

"Yep." Her brow was firm, and her jaw tense.

She wasn't okay at all, but she was going to fake it. He had to give her some credit for being stoic. Bennett just hoped they didn't regret it.

Stephanie unlocked the door and jerked it open. "Bennett, when all of that happened here yesterday —oh. Annie's here already." Her head whipped around as a small coupe pulled into the lot and parked next to her truck.

Bennett watched as a young woman stepped out of the driver's door. Even at just a glance, she looked much the way Stephanie had when she was younger. Bright and beautiful, she gave her mom a smile and Bennett a quizzical look before she opened the back door and unloaded three dogs. "Good boys! Such good babies!"

The largest dog, a big hound, quivered as he sniffed the air and assessed Bennett.

"Sherlock gets a little nervous," Stephanie

explained. "He's new to the group and still trying to figure things out."

But as Annie walked over to them, Sherlock suddenly put his ears back and wagged his tail. He wiggled like crazy as he strained against his collar and tried to get to Bennett.

"I think he likes you!" Annie laughed.

"Definitely. Annie, this is an old friend of mine, Bennett. He's going to be hanging out here at the clinic today."

"Nice to meet you. Are you a vet, too?" Annie reached out her hand.

Bennett shook it over Sherlock's head while the dog continued to love on him. "No."

"Yes," Stephanie replied at the same time. "I mean, he's interested in veterinary medicine."

He could see that Stephanie was struggling through this one. They should've talked about it on the way there, but they'd been caught up in everything else. "I'm just doing some research."

"That's exciting! On what specifically?"

"Ah..." Bennett struggled to remember something Stephanie had said about her practice. He'd been listening, but it all escaped him at the moment.

"Integrative medicine in general," Stephanie

supplied, waving everyone in the back door. "It's for a magazine article."

"Nice. I look forward to reading it." Annie gave him a curious look before she took the dogs around the corner from the exam rooms and into the office area. She unclipped them from their leashes, which she hung on a hook. "Mom, what happened with that wolf last night? I should've asked you about that before I brought the dogs in here."

"Oh, no. It's fine. It all worked out." Stephanie made a show of putting her things away and getting ready for the day. "I reached out to Cindy, you know, my friend who works for a wildlife rescue? Once I got the wolf stabilized, she was able to take him."

"That's great! Is he going to be okay?" Annie fired up the computer and turned on the lights in the lobby.

"Yeah. I think he's going to be just fine." Stephanie met Bennett's eyes, her lips in a tight smile and her brows up as if to say she was doing her best.

Annie turned to Bennett. "It's too bad you weren't here yesterday. That wolf would've been a pretty exciting topic for a magazine article."

"Yes, that really is too bad." Now, it was Bennett's turn to smile at Stephanie. They were dancing all around it. He knew none of it sounded very natural, but Annie would never guess the truth. No one would.

Stephanie sat down in front of the computer and looked through the appointments for the day. "Let's see. Looks like Mrs. Pratchett has the first appointment for her Yorkie's acupuncture treatment. Could you ready Exam One for that, please?"

"Acupuncture for dogs, hm? I'd be interested in seeing that," Bennett commented, remembering the little gold needles that'd been in the back of his neck the day before.

"I don't think that'll be a problem," Stephanie replied with a knowing smile. "Annie, we've got Porkchop coming in right after that, but it's just for his regular shots. Do you think you can handle that? Then I'll just pop in and check on him right after I'm done with the acupuncture."

"Sure thing." Annie headed off down the hallway.

"I hope you won't be too bored following me around all day," Stephanie said quietly when they were alone. "The magazine thing was the best idea I could come up with."

"It gives me an excuse to be near you, and that's

all I need." It was honest to a fault, but he could hardly help himself when it came to her.

And as the day went on, Bennett almost wished he really was a journalist of some sort. Stephanie was kind and gentle with every patient, and she explained each procedure thoroughly to the animal's owner both before she began and during the process. He hadn't even known about these naturopathic remedies before, but he probably wouldn't have given them a second thought if he hadn't seen that every one of Stephanie's patients left the office looking much better than they had when they'd come in.

Then there was Annie. It was odd to know that Stephanie had a child with another man, a child that could've been his if he'd only made different decisions. Whatever regrets he had were quickly overtaken by the sheer delight of being around these two women. They laughed and joked, easing into their normal routine despite his presence. Annie looked up to her mother, listening carefully and taking her work there seriously. They obviously had a great relationship. Bennett knew that he'd hurt Stephanie when he'd left her, but he took comfort in knowing she had such happiness in her daughter.

7

"I'm just so worried about her. I know something must be wrong." Mrs. Cabrera fretfully stroked the little border collie mix's head, smoothing back the swirl of black and white fur.

Stephanie knew there was some advice patients simply didn't want to hear. She still had to tell them, though. "I'll be honest. Sundae here is pretty overweight. That's the first thing my mind goes to when you tell me she's struggling to get up."

"But she burns up so much energy when she's running around in the yard, and then she's always hungry. I don't really feed her that much," Mrs. Cabrera protested. "I think it's just her natural body shape."

"It's very easy to overfeed our house pets," Stephanie replied. "We can get you in for some nutrition counseling."

"I don't think she needs anything like that," the woman answered quickly. "There's no reason she has to look like a bikini model."

Stephanie refrained from arguing with her. The results would come from concrete testing, probably the only thing that would make this woman understand what she was doing to her dog. "We're going to start with some X-rays to eliminate any fractures or things of that nature. My assistant and I will take Sundae into the back, and we'll have her ready to head home in just a minute."

"I don't think she'll sit still." Mrs. Cabrera scrunched her fingers through Sundae's fur. "She's a very nervous dog, you know."

"She'll do just fine." Stephanie put her arms under the dog and scooped her off the exam table, causing Sundae to issue a groan of discomfort.

Bennett followed her out into the hallway. "It seems like you have to comfort the owners just as much as the animals."

"You're not wrong," she replied with a smile. "People don't want to hear that their pet is overweight because it means the blame is on them. The thing is, it's not really about blame. It's about doing what's best for the animal. If this girl doesn't drop a few pounds, she'll only continue to struggle. I'll get her sorted out, though."

"You're impressive to watch, you know. You have a lot more patience than most."

Stephanie laughed. "Either that comes from being in the business, or it was something I already had before I started. Regardless, it's pretty necessary."

"Yes, I can see that. I don't think I could do what you do, but I'm sure I'll write a fascinating article about it." Bennett had already made friends with Sundae at the beginning of the exam when the dog had surprised her owner by wiggling her way right over to him to say hi, even though she was supposedly terrified of strangers, particularly men. He reached up and scratched her nose, making her close her eyes in pleasure.

"I think you've got a knack for this, too. All these dogs are crazy about you." She knew it really wasn't just coincidence, either. Stephanie hadn't told him yet about her psychic ability. She almost had on the way there, but when circumstances had stopped her, she'd let it go. Bennett had shared one hell of a secret with her about who he was, but this was a secret that Stephanie sometimes still doubted herself. She saw the flashes of imagery and felt the emotions of the animals around her. It was a lot of what made her good at her job. With the lack of concrete evidence that she was doing it right, though, it wasn't easy to talk about.

If she had even the slightest bit of talent, it showed every time one of these animals was around Bennett. Rambo emanated warm fuzzy feelings every time he saw his owner, but it didn't have to be an animal who knew Bennett well for her to pick up on these reactions. Sherlock had been thrilled to see him when they arrived, and Stephanie was quite convinced that he recognized Bennett as the wolf in the woods. Sundae adored him, and even a cat that'd been in earlier that morning was more comfortable getting out of his cage for Bennett than he was for his owner.

"Hey." Annie stepped out of an exam room, the whiff of sterilization products following her. "I've got this one all ready to go. Doing an X-ray?"

"Yeah, can you help?" Though it was possible to do it alone, Stephanie preferred to have help. It would give the best results and be safest for the dog.

"Of course."

"Bennett, if you don't mind, I need someone trained on this. You can wait in the office if you like, or you can go make friends with everyone in the lobby. I'm sure they'll all be happier to see you than anyone else."

"Sure thing." He gave her one last smile before he retreated down the hallway.

"What's going on with this sweet little thing?" Annie held open the door to the back room where they kept their larger equipment and then shut it once Stephanie was inside.

"Her legs are hurting her."

"I think I can see why. You're a pudgy little baby, aren't you?" Annie held out her hand for Sundae to sniff before she stroked her fur. "Just a chunky monkey, huh?"

"Don't say any of that in front of her human," Stephanie said with a laugh as she let Annie take Sundae and began setting everything up. "She's convinced it's something else, but we'll see what the X-ray says. She's also worried about Sundae sitting still."

"Sundae? Oh, that's the cutest name! I can see why, too. This little swirl of brown on her head against the white makes her look like a hot fudge sundae. And she's going to be good, aren't you? You look like a smart girl. Come here." Annie put her on the table and put on her protective vest.

"We'll start her out on her side. Perfect." Stephanie put on her vest as well.

"Hey, Mom?"

"Hm?"

"Have I told you what a terrible liar you are?"

Stephanie blinked and swung her head over to look at her daughter. "Excuse me?"

Annie laughed. "Come on. I don't need your psychic abilities to know that this Bennett guy isn't just some old friend of yours."

"He is, though," Stephanie protested. "I've known him since high school."

"Okay, I'll give you that." Annie placed a marker down near Sundae's feet so they'd be able to tell later which side of the dog they were looking at on the X-ray. "Good girl. Stay."

The machine clicked and whirred.

"But even if you did know him back then, you can't seriously expect me to believe that he's some sort of journalist. He looks like he spends a lot more time at the gym than behind a computer, and I haven't seen him take a single note since he's been here." Annie encouraged Sundae to get up and then lay down on her other side so they could be sure they had a good image of her whole body.

Stephanie's hands were on autopilot as she did her work. It was a good thing since her mind was floundering. It wasn't like she could tell Annie the truth about Bennett. There wasn't a single bit of that truth that would sound any better than the lies she'd already committed herself to. A wave of guilt came along with that. Shit. She hadn't really meant to lie to her own daughter. Annie wasn't a kid anymore, and she'd understand plenty as an adult. Still, all of this business with Bennett was a lot, even for Stephanie to comprehend.

"Then there's the way he looks at you," Annie continued as she changed out the marker. "That alone is enough to make me think there's more here than a professional relationship."

Annie was the only person who knew about the unique way Stephanie could communicate with animals. "Looks at me how?"

"Oh, you know. Like you're some lost treasure, and he's been searching all the ancient temples in the world for you. Good girl, Sundae." Annie gently lowered the dog to the ground and watched her walk around the room, cautiously sniffing.

"Really? I think you've been watching too many

late-night movies." Stephanie shut off the machine, feeling her face heat as she realized just how she and Bennett must appear. She'd seen all those looks from Bennett, of course, but she hadn't realized they were so obvious to anyone else. What must her clients have thought? Hopefully, they were more focused on their pets.

"Don't be weird, Mom. You guys like each other. That's okay. There's no reason to hide it." Annie opened the treat jar, took out the smallest one she could find, and offered it to Sundae. The dog looked up at her with forlorn eyes for a moment, white rimming the deep brown irises, and then gingerly took the tidbit from her hand.

Stephanie let out a sigh as she watched Sundae move through the room, analyzing her for any signs of illness or injury. The computer was working on the images, which would be ready shortly, but simply observing the patient could tell her a lot. "I'm sorry, Annie. I didn't mean to deceive you. The whole thing is new to me, and I haven't had much time to think about it."

"I guess that means you've finally forgiven me for going on that date with Travis Hanson when I told you I was at the movies with Courtney?" Annie teased.

"Yes, I suppose so," Stephanie laughed, though she hadn't thought about that in a very long time. "But only if you'll forgive me. I don't know exactly what's happening between Bennett and I, so it's difficult to explain."

"There's no explanation necessary, really," Annie reasoned. She bent down and scratched her fingers through the dog's thick fur. "You deserve some happiness after what happened with Dad."

"I don't know about that," Stephanie hedged. She checked the computer, wanting to return to Mrs. Cabrera with the X-rays ready. "That was a long time ago, and it doesn't really affect me anymore."

"Sure it does," Annie insisted. "You're not angry at each other, and I can't complain about that. I was always glad that you guys didn't have a bitter divorce. Going back and forth between you two was easier than what other kids I knew had to go through. That makes it sound like it's all hunky dory, but what about you?"

"What about me? Ah, here they are." The images had finished processing, and she looked them over. Nothing was there that indicated any skeletal issues with Sundae. There could still be a swollen tendon or some nerve damage, so she'd have to investigate further to find out for sure.

"You've never done anything for yourself," Annie explained. "You were either involved in your work and developing your practice, or you were taking care of me and being a good mom. As far as I know, you've never really dated anyone else after you and Dad split up. Unless there's something else you're hiding from me, young lady." She gave her mother a mock, stern look.

"No, ma'am," Stephanie replied innocently. Or at least she wasn't hiding anything that was her secret to tell. "I'd better get Sundae back to her owner. I'm going to double-check for any inflammation issues I might've missed, but I still think my first diagnosis was the correct one."

"Okay." Annie handed the leash over. "You know, I think I want to keep the dogs at my place again tonight."

Stephanie studied her carefully. "Why? I know they've got to be a handful for you."

Annie lifted a shoulder. "I like their company. Gotta go up to the front and see if anyone needs to be checked in now!" Without giving her mother another chance to reply or argue, she flitted off toward the front of the building.

"Everything go all right?" Bennett rejoined her in the hall.

"Well enough." There was no time to tell him about Annie's suspicions. He came with her into the exam room and sat down, observing just as he'd promised to do even though he definitely wasn't a journalist.

"She was an absolute doll," Stephanie began as she shut the door behind her. "She listens wonderfully to voice commands, and you can tell she truly wants to behave well."

Mrs. Cabrera straightened in her chair and wiggled her head slightly. "I do spend a lot of time with her."

Which was great, but they needed less of that time to be spent eating. "The X-ray shows that her skeletal system is strong and intact. That leaves us with a few other options to explore. She could have some inflammation, and in that case, I'd recommend acupuncture and massage." She went on, discussing all the various possibilities for Sundae while she palpated her joints and flexed her legs, checking for anything she might've missed, but her mind was still on Bennett and what Annie had said.

She couldn't deny her connection to Bennett even after all this time. It shouldn't be there. Considering how young they were when they'd been together, it seemed they'd lived an entire lifetime apart. Yet, her body, mind, and soul had other things to say about it. She was there for her clients and their pets, but Stephanie remained intrinsically aware of Bennett the entire time. Was that the whole fated thing Bennett had told her about? It'd sure worked to get her into bed before, not that it would've taken much in the first place. Bennett was damn hot, and the attraction was much more than a pretty face. He set her on fire with every touch. He spoke to her and looked at her as though he truly wanted her. Annie's little analogy about lost treasure wasn't entirely off-par. There was a lot of lost time that they could've been enjoying each other.

Unfortunately, even though he'd left her entire body buzzing, she couldn't think about Bennett without acknowledging the reality of their situation. He was there not because he was writing an article, and not because he just wanted to spend time with her. His enemies were now her enemies. Did that mean they were about to become Annie's enemies as well? It gave her a lot to think about, though it'd been much more pleasant when she could just think about how incredible Bennett looked naked.

"Well, all right," Mrs. Cabrera agreed reluctantly. "I did come here looking for something other than just your typical vet, so I suppose I can't turn my nose up completely at nutrition counseling."

"I appreciate that," Stephanie said honestly. She'd been unable to find any other issues with the dog, and her official diagnosis was that the sweet little girl simply resembled her name a bit too closely. "The truth is that any medical problem Sundae may be having will only be exacerbated by excess weight. This will be good for her no matter what. We'll just step up front and make some appointments for you."

"What do you think, Sundae? Well, I think I'll have to just leave her here with you!" Mrs. Cabrera laughed as she realized while the adults were talking, Sundae had made a pillow of Bennett's shoe and fallen fast asleep.

"Are you doing okay?" Bennett asked when they'd finished up and were alone for a moment in the office. "You seemed all perky and happy, and then it just dropped off. Did something happen?"

What any woman in America wouldn't give for a man who picked up on her feelings like that! Stephanie wondered if this had anything to do with him being a shifter and if there was a certain animal instinct that went along with it. She'd be asking him an awful lot of questions once they'd made it through the day. "I just need to take care of something. Excuse me for a second."

She found Annie cleaning and disinfecting the exam room that Sundae and Mrs. Cabrera had occupied just a few minutes ago. Annie was always right on top of things. It was something Stephanie appreciated as her boss, but it also made her proud as her mother. "I had an idea."

"What's that?" Annie spritzed down the exam table.

"You keep saying that you and your friends want to go on a shopping trip to Portland. I think you should go." Getting out of town would likely be much safer for Annie than staying in Eugene. It was one thing for Stephanie's life to be on the line, but it was completely different when it was her daughter's.

Annie paused and gave her mom a keen stare. "If anything, I thought maybe *you* should be going out of town. You know, a romantic weekend getaway?"

Bennett's place was so remote that it was almost like a getaway itself. Though the numerous security measures he'd taken were a bit disturbing, Stephanie rather liked the idea of being completely alone with him. This wasn't about that, though. "No, I mean it. You work hard around here, and I think you should treat yourself a little."

"What about the dogs?" Annie gestured with her head toward the office. "I already told you I was going to take them tonight."

"That's fine. I'll just swing by and grab them on my lunch break tomorrow. It sounds like the best of both worlds to me." Not everything in life could be so finely balanced, but Stephanie could see no reason why it wouldn't work.

8

"I REALLY DON'T LIKE THIS."

"I know." Stephanie put her hand on Bennett's arm as he pulled into the parking lot behind the clinic the next morning. "You'll watch me get inside safely, though."

"Really, Stephanie." He pulled to a stop and put his SUV in park. They'd left her truck at his place this time since his vehicle was equipped with all the right remotes to make getting in and out of his property easier. "Every fiber of my being is telling me I can't just leave you here."

"And then we're left with the same problem we had before. I can't just shut the whole place down, Bennett. This is the sort of job that you work rain or shine, sick or healthy, death threats or no death threats," Stephanie reasoned, though her voice shook a little on that last part. "I was open yesterday, and nothing happened."

"I was here with you yesterday," he reminded her. Bennett put his hand under her chin and grazed his finger along her jawline, taking her in. If he had his way, they wouldn't have to worry about the Bloodmoon Crew or her business. They could just hide away from the world for days, doing nothing but enjoying each other. That wasn't realistic, though, and abandoning her practice wouldn't make her happy. Could he make her happy?

She smiled at him sleepily. They hadn't exactly had much time to get a good night's rest. "I'll do everything just like we said. I'll keep the door locked and only let in clients I know. Everyone else will just have to go elsewhere because we're short on staff. Which is true since Annie won't be here today."

He was grateful that she was trying to appease him and his worries, but Stephanie could never really know what she did to him. As a human, she would never understand the demand of his wolf to keep her safe. It all sounded like a good plan to her, but Bennett could see nothing but flaws. "You could always just come to the packhouse with me."

"I don't think that's a good idea." She pulled

away from his hand to take a deep breath. "I'm not saying never. I know that's a big part of your life and who you are. I just don't know if I'm ready for it yet, and I really do have a lot of work today. It'll be all right, Bennett."

Damn it. If she just kept saying his name like that, he'd do damn near anything she pleased. "Fine. I'll make this as quick as possible, and then I'll be back. If anything seems off, even just a little out of the ordinary, then call me."

"I will." She leaned in to give him a slow, languorous kiss that tempted him to lock the doors and drive immediately back home.

Bennett waited until she'd gone through the back door, and he knew it was shut. Then he waited a bit longer, just to be sure. His wolf was pissed. It didn't like this any more than he did. Bennett had a feeling it wouldn't appreciate the next thing he was about to do, either.

He turned south. How long had it been since he'd visited the Glenwood packhouse? His work kept him busy enough that he didn't make it to many meetings. Even when he did, he already felt like he was on the outskirts of the pack. His skills were useful, so it wasn't like his Alpha and the other leaders of the pack didn't call on his help every now and then, but he knew his hands were stained.

The low clouds were drizzling consistently by the time he pulled up to the big, cedar-sided home backed by acres and acres of woods. Bennett had spent plenty of time there when he was younger. It was always a treat when his father had business there and he got to play with the Glenwood boys and the other young shifters. This was the one place in the world where they never had to worry about being their true selves.

But it was different for Stephanie. She'd been honest enough to say she was uncertain about diving headlong into the shifter world. It'd surprised him a bit, since she'd fired off round after round of questions the previous night once they'd gotten back to his place. As far as Bennett could tell, she was fascinated by the whole idea. That didn't erase the fact that his parents had been blatantly against their relationship. How much was that knowledge affecting her?

He stepped up to the front door, where Brody greeted him. "Hey, Ben. Long time, no see." The pack's third in command reached out and pulled Bennett in to slap his back.

"I always hated it when you called me that."

Bennett stepped into the living room. The Glen-woods had been a strong pack for many years, and it showed in the framed original artwork and gleaming hardwood floors. He'd certainly had some of this in mind when he'd built his own place.

"I know. That's exactly why I kept doing it," Brody replied with a grin. "Rex is expecting you. He's in his den."

"What kind of mood is he in?" Bennett asked. He eyed the tattoos on Brody's arms, thinking it was about time he got a little new ink himself. Once life settled down, of course, which it never did.

Brody lifted his brows. "Is this something that serious?"

Bennett thought about Stephanie, working all alone at the clinic, vulnerable to the Bloodmoon Crew. They were already a problem for him before, but the issue had grown far more vital now that she was involved. "I think so."

"Well, you know Rex. He's always got his plate full, but he likes that. He's been working a lot with the new Alpha of the Morwoods to get them all straightened out." Brody motioned toward the door. "I've got to get back home, but I'll catch you later."

"See ya." Bennett headed through the living room and turned down the hall. He knew this house as though it were his own. In many ways, it was. The Glenwood pack had always been a generous and charitable one. Empty rooms were always ready for anyone in need. He and his mother had stayed in some themselves shortly after the restaurant had burned down, when they'd needed to be around their pack more than anything. He needed them again now.

The door was open, and he knocked on the frame.

Rex sat at his desk, frowning at his computer. The consistent drizzle moved in waves down the window behind him. As soon as he saw Bennett in the doorway, the Alpha got up and came around the desk. "Bennett. Good to see you, man. I have to admit I was kind of surprised when you asked to meet with me. Have a seat. I'd offer you a whiskey if it wasn't so early in the day." He led the way to the two armchairs in front of the fireplace. It wasn't cold enough yet for the fire to be lit, but it still created a cozy corner in his den.

"No worries. Sorry for such short notice." He sat, remembering when he and Rex were too young for this room to mean anything more than the place where adults talked about boring stuff. "It really couldn't wait."

"It's not a problem," Rex assured him. "I spend at least a few days a week here for pack business and try to split my time the best I can with Selene's. I've been busy, so it's been difficult to finalize it, but I think I've got it all down. Anyway, you didn't come here to talk about my rock club."

"No," Bennett agreed. "I need to talk to you about the Bloodmoon Crew."

Rex was sitting back in his armchair, looking relaxed, but his shoulders tensed slightly at the mention of the name. "The leadership of the Silvergrove pack? I haven't heard anything about them in a long time."

"Well, they haven't exactly been staying underground if you know what you're looking for. Their activity has picked up lately. They've been all over town, pushing drugs, selling weapons, and demanding protection payments." His wolf roiled angrily inside him. The bastards were everywhere, and he was out there in the woods sitting on his ass. Bennett should be doing something about it. He reminded himself that coming out there to talk to Rex *was* doing something about it, but he worried it wouldn't be enough.

Rex put his elbow on the arm of the chair and ran his thumb just under his lips. "Can I assume there's a reason you're taking a particular interest in them right now?"

"Work," Bennett replied simply. "I was hired by a member of the Silvergroves to take them out. They're running their pack into the ground, threatening their own members, and worse. They came to me, and I took the job. The problem is that the Crew has grown much more powerful over the years. I can't take them out alone."

"Are you asking me what I think you're asking me?" Rex asked slowly, his blue eyes burning into Bennett's.

"I am. I need the pack's help. The Bloodmoon Crew has already tried to exact their revenge on me. They left me for dead, and I probably wouldn't be here if it weren't for some lucky circumstances." He'd save the part about letting his shifter secret out for later. Rex was obviously already on edge. "There are more members than there used to be, and they've been at this long enough to know what they're doing. The job is too big for one person, but it will save many lives once it's done."

Rex's nostrils flared as he pulled in a deep breath and let it out as a sigh. He steepled his fingers together, holding them just under his chin. "Bennett, you know the Glenwood history with the Bloodmoon Crew as well as I do. My father was Alpha when they burned down your dad's restaurant. We evened it out when we came after them at that little dive bar they were operating. He was careful to ensure that we didn't go over the top, taking out the same amount of damage and lives that Nelson and his men had. It was a show of force, one that let the Silvergroves know that we meant business. My father and Nelson made a truce, and we haven't had any trouble with them since then."

"I'm aware of that." Not that Bennett thought they could ever truly do enough to exact revenge for his losses, and he sure as shit didn't need the history lesson.

"Then you understand there's nothing I can do," Rex concluded, his jaw firm. "It was decided long ago that they would leave us alone, and we would leave them alone."

Bennett sat forward. "You don't really mean that, do you?"

"I wasn't Alpha back then, and it wasn't a decision I made, but it was decided by my father. I have to stand by that." Rex dropped his hands to his knees. "And I expect you to understand it. Unless you want to take it up with Jimmy himself."

"Come on, Rex. The Glenwoods are a strong

pack. We take care of our own. If someone is hungry, we feed them. If they need a place to stay, we make sure it happens. I know all about that big supply closet your mom has in the basement so that she can help the needy at every turn." He was on the edge of his seat now.

"Is there a direct danger to this pack?" Rex asked carefully.

"Not that I'm aware of," Bennett was forced to admit. "They're after me, but I'm not counting that."

"I get it, Bennett. I do. But I'm not going to violate a treaty our pack made simply because *you* decided you wanted to take this job." Rex pointed a firm finger of blame at him.

"It's what I do for a living, in case you've forgotten. The police department and their purchased pawns didn't want me to help the public unless it was all within their special little parameters, and you're starting to sound an awful lot like them." He rose from his seat and swept a hand through his hair, trying to control his anger.

"Don't give me that bullshit, Bennett." Now Rex was on his feet as well, his hands on his hips as he stared Bennett down. "You didn't take that job because of any moral obligation, and you didn't even take it for the money. You've been waiting to exact your personal revenge on the Bloodmoons, and you jumped at the chance."

"My family's business is gone. My sister is gone. My father is gone. All I got out of that is some dumbass contract. Is that supposed to make me feel better, Rex?" Bennett could feel himself losing control as all the anger and sadness of those days came rushing back to him. "Was that ever supposed to be enough?"

"It had to be enough to make sure we didn't end up in a war with them," Rex snapped. "The Glenwoods weren't strong enough for that at the time, and it was the best option possible. I'm not going to just turn around and authorize everyone to come after the Silvergroves as revenge for something we already repaid them for."

"Fine." A sense of calm determination settled down on Bennett's shoulders. "I'll handle it myself, just as I always have."

"No, you won't," Rex replied as Bennett turned for the door. "You shouldn't have taken that job in the first place, and you need to stand down."

Bennett turned. "You can't be serious, Rex. I took the job, and I'm going to follow through with it."

"Bennett." Rex's face was hard and serious as he closed the gap between them. His shoulders were back, and his eyes bored straight into Bennett's. "I command you, as your Alpha, to stand down and call off this job against the Bloodmoon Crew."

It was like a punch in the gut, though Rex hadn't touched him at all. Bennett felt his wolf cowering in submission. The Alpha command couldn't be ignored, and he had no choice. "Damn you," he whispered.

"It's for your own good as well as everyone else's." Rex turned and crossed the room to his desk. "Any kind of rash action is a mistake if they're truly that strong, as is the violation of an agreement. I can send a few guards for protection if you'd like, or I can try to talk this through with Nelson, but that's as far as I can go."

"Don't bother." Bennett turned and stormed out of the den. What the hell was he thinking, going there and asking Rex for help? He knew about that fucking truce. Why should he believe it would be any different simply because some time had passed and a new Glenwood Alpha was in place? Rex had not only denied him any assistance in taking down the Bloodmoon Crew, but he'd also forced Bennett to stop pursuing them. It didn't matter that Bennett had been hired for this job. He'd received the Alpha command, and he had to obey.

As he sped back into town, his mind was working toward another solution. There had to be one. There had to be some way around this.

The full moon hung in the morning sky, remaining though the day had started. Their pack had kept the old tradition of worshipping the goddess Selene, who now looked down upon him with her pale, translucent eyes. Rex's mate, Lori, the pack Luna, was a descendent of hers. Selene had blessed the Glenwoods many times, and her power could alter the flow of time and bring light into darkness. "I don't know how much you can help me now," he said as he sped along the highway, "but I sure could use it. I can put my life on the line, but now I've put Stephanie's right there alongside mine. I can't disobey my Alpha, but there has to be something I can do."

9

WHETHER IT WAS BENEVOLENT INSPIRATION FROM Selene or his own revelation, Bennett would never know, but he found himself pulling up in front of the police station next. His wolf churned in irritation. He shouldn't be there, where he wasn't welcome. He should also be getting back to Stephanie. He'd left her alone so he could run his errand, one that hadn't yet come to fruition. Was she okay? He checked his phone but saw no calls or messages.

He stepped into the lobby and was met with a surprised look from the service clerk. "Bennett."

"Hi, Jeanette." She'd started working at the station when her husband had passed suddenly. At the time, she'd said it was just something temporary to help fill the void. Her father had been a police officer when she was a girl, and working there felt familiar. That was ten years ago, and she was still there.

"Are you all right?" she asked. "You look a little out of sorts."

"I definitely feel it," he agreed, wondering just how much his stress was showing on the outside. Jeanette had always been very compassionate, though, wanting to take care of the officers and detectives as much as they'd allow her to. "It doesn't help that I'm here, either."

"Hey, at least you're on the right side of the cuffs," she joked. "There's been some turnover in staffing if you know what I mean. If that makes you feel any better."

"A bit." He'd heard some of the higher-ups who'd terminated him were no longer on the force, having moved off to bigger and better jobs. Their way to them was no doubt greased by the Bloodmoon Crew, so they still couldn't be up to any good. "Is Kane Glenwood in?" He could've just called, but Bennett knew this was the sort of conversation he needed to have in person.

"You've caught him at his desk, actually. I'll buzz you back." With a smile, she hit the button.

Walking through that door was like traveling

through time. At one point, Bennett had known this station like the back of his hand. Every desk and face were familiar, and he'd been able to operate the coffee machine with his eyes closed. He very well might have done so a time or two while working late. It all felt foreign now, like dreaming of a home you can never truly go back to. Bennett felt the curious stares as he made his way toward Kane's desk.

He took in the empty coffee cups, the scattered papers, and the thick file folders. "I see nothing has changed around here."

Kane looked up from his work and grinned. "Not much. It's the same old grind."

"I figured. And you're the best sucker they've got to work your life away at it."

"You know it." Kane held up his hands as he accepted his fate. He glanced to the side, noticing they were getting some attention, and lowered his voice. "I'm a little surprised you're willing to show your face around here, considering what happened."

Bennett knew Kane didn't hold any grudges against him for that. As part of the Glenwood pack, Kane understood more of what was happening than most other officers around them. "I'm not willing to do it for long. Are you free to go for a ride? I've got some information I'd like to unload on you."

"I was just about to head out on my break, actually." Kane stood up and grabbed his keys. "I'll drive."

"If you insist." They went out the side door to the private lot, and Bennett followed him to his squad car.

"I ought to insist you ride in the back," Kane cracked.

It felt a little too familiar getting into the front seat of a squad car. With Kane, though, it was a comfortable feeling. "It's been a minute."

"Sure has," Kane agreed. "Whatever you've got to talk about must be big for you to come all the way into the station."

"Nah, I just missed the donuts," Bennett replied dryly. "I just came from a visit with Rex."

Kane raised his dark brows in surprise as he pulled up against the curb near First Light Café. "That's not like you."

"I know." Bennett waited for the rest of the story until they were seated in the little restaurant.

Tiffany Fairmount, the proprietor and now part of their pack since she was mated to Declan Ridgefield, came to take their order. "What can I get you boys today?"

"Coffee and whatever delicious muffin you've got

in stock," Kane replied. "I don't even care what flavor."

"Can do. How about you, Bennett?" Tiffany turned to him.

"Um, just coffee is fine."

She gave him a curious look, clearly wanting to feed him. "I've been working on some new breakfast sandwiches that I need someone to try out for me. You fellas wanna be my guinea pigs?"

"Sure," Kane replied for both of them.

"I'm surprised she even remembers who I am," Bennett commented as Tiffany left to get their order.

Kane shrugged. "From what I've seen, that's just who she is. She knows all of her customers, their allergies, and their kids. There's no reason why she shouldn't know everyone in our pack, even if you don't hang around very much."

"There you go." Tiffany returned quickly. "Roasted turkey, eggs, spinach, and just a bit of cheese on whole wheat. I think it still needs something else, but you let me know. And your muffin, of course." With a wink, she was back in the kitchen.

"All right." Kane picked up his sandwich and eyed it with interest. "Tell me what's going on."

Bennett left his sandwich on the plate for the moment. "It's about the Bloodmoon Crew."

"Isn't that old business by now?" Kane lifted the bread and peered under it. He took a big bite and sank back in his seat.

"You'd think so, but they're active again," Bennett explained. "They're stronger than ever. They've got eyes everywhere, and they're dangerous as hell. I've been hired to take them out."

Kane stared at him for a moment before he swallowed. "Are you serious?"

"Deadly." His stomach growled, so Bennett picked up the sandwich. They didn't have time to be sitting around at a café. He should've just insisted that they speak quickly in the parking lot so he could get back to Stephanie. His wolf was getting testy, certain he was doing the wrong thing. The sandwich was damn good, though.

"I'm not surprised you took the job," Kane replied, "but it sure isn't going to be easy."

"It hasn't been." Bennett quickly recited his first attempt. "I knew they were strong, but it's gotten worse. I've seen evidence of just how much chaos they're causing in Eugene, but Nelson Silvergrove is smart enough to lay low. He's keeping everything mild enough that it's not on the cops' radar."

"You're right about that," Kane confirmed with a nod. "No one has mentioned them or anything like that in a long time. It's all traffic tickets, drug offenses, burglaries, and the occasional murder."

"Some of that, no doubt, has to do with the Bloodmoon Crew, even if they've made it look otherwise," Bennett asserted. "They've grown too damn powerful for me to take down by myself. I've got an extra problem, too. I've met my mate along the way."

"Well, shit!" Kane reached across the table and clapped him on the shoulder. "It's about damn time. Congratulations."

"I should say I've rediscovered her," Bennett corrected himself. "It's Stephanie, the girl I dated in high school. Do you remember her?"

"Oh, yeah." Kane set down his sandwich long enough to wipe his hands and get a drink. "I hadn't thought about all that drama in a long time. You two had quite the Romeo and Juliet thing going."

"And we're going to get the same ending, if things don't change soon. They've already come after Stephanie and me once. That's why I went to see Rex this morning. I wanted his help." Disappointment washed over him anew.

Kane polished off his sandwich. "And what did my cousin have to say about that?"

"Damn near the same thing the chief of police told

me when I tried to pursue them several years ago," Bennett replied with a growl. "I don't get it, Kane. These bastards keep popping up in my life, but my hands get tied every time. I couldn't take them down through my police work, and then I got fired for pursuing them on the side. I went to Rex for help, hoping the Glenwoods as a whole could finally solve this problem. He not only refused to help, but he forbade me from even finishing the job on my own with an Alpha command."

"Ouch." Kane took a long sip of his coffee. "I know Rex wouldn't do such a thing without good reason."

"That's the problem with him, isn't it? There's always reason and logic. I get it, Kane. I really do. He has a lot on his plate, and he can't just fly off the handle if he's going to run a successful pack. But this is getting critical. If the Bloodmoon Crew is allowed to continue, they'll suddenly be a much bigger problem than anyone realized." He could see it all unfolding, but why couldn't anyone else?

"I talked with him about it back when you were having your troubles with the police force." Kane put his coffee down and picked up his muffin. He broke it in half and studied the inside. "Cranberry walnut. Anyway, I know about the agreement Jimmy had made with Nelson. I'm guessing that's why Rex isn't helping?"

"Right." Bennett realized he was gripping the handle of his coffee mug a bit too hard and set it down. "He actually offered to go talk it over with Nelson. The only thing that will do is make it worse."

"I know it's frustrating, but don't underestimate Rex's negotiating skills. It's hard when we don't have the chance to just eliminate our enemies, but we should be grateful that we have an Alpha who actually wants to slow things down and talk. That's a good part of why the Glenwoods have been so successful. Our leaders don't just fly off the handle." Kane took another bite of his muffin. "Damn, this is good."

Bennett sighed. "I take it you're on his side."

"Don't put it that way. I definitely sympathize with your cause. Your mate could be in danger. I'm guessing Rex offered some guards?" Kane raised a brow.

"He did." Not that Bennett had been willing to accept them.

"Then take them. Know that you have some protection for her, even if it dings your pride a bit. It's the best option you have right now." Kane pulled his wallet out and left several bills on the table.

"It's not good enough." Bennett shook his head. "I've got to do more, but I don't know what. I've worked my way out of some pretty tough situations, but this one just feels impossible."

"I wish I knew of a way to help you." Kane's blue eyes met his. "I don't want to go against what Rex has already told you, especially since it was an Alpha command. No offense, but you already lost your job on the force over this. I've got a kid to take care of, and I can't afford to have the same thing happen to me. Unless something comes along in some sort of official capacity, I feel like my hands are tied."

"Yeah. I know." Bennett drummed his hands on the countertop. He'd known when he'd come to see him that Kane would have to follow the rules. He bent a few here and there to accommodate for the shifter world, but he could only go so far.

"Central dispatch to five-oh-four." The radio on Kane's shoulder buzzed to life.

He tapped the button. "Five-oh-four, go ahead."

"We've got an emergency call from the vet clinic out on Barger."

Bennett's heart nearly jumped out of his mouth. "That's it. That's Stephanie's clinic."

"This is five-oh-four. I'm on my way." Kane was out of his seat. "Looks like you've got the official capacity you were hoping for."

As they raced to the scene, Bennett only hoped they could get there in time.

10

"I can fit you in on Thursday afternoon at two o'clock. How does that work with your schedule?" Stephanie sat in front of her computer, having run to the office right after finishing up with a client. She'd built this place from the ground up, and she was used to doing every job and any job. Sometimes, she brought in temps or other help, but for the most part, it was just herself and Annie. She easily flicked through the appointment system on the computer. "All right. I've got you set up. We'll see you on Thursday."

Hanging up, Stephanie headed back into the exam room where she'd just finished a cold laser treatment for an old hound with arthritis. It hadn't turned him into a young pup again, but he was decidedly better than before they'd started these sessions. Stephanie smiled to herself as she cleaned and sanitized the space. It was quiet that day, not having a lobby full of hopeful walk-ins. She'd politely kept to just her previously set appointments, and even though it kept her hopping from room to room, she was truly enjoying herself. She took care of each patient from start to finish, finding the joy in her work all over again.

It was just too bad that it'd only come about because of Bennett's concerns. There'd been no doubt that those wolves they'd encountered the day before wanted to hurt them. She couldn't ignore that, though the peace of the clinic right now made it easy to try. If someone was going to come after her, why wouldn't they have done it already? Why would they wait, especially if they were these highly skilled shifters who ran a crime syndicate that even the police couldn't pursue?

"You're just trying to use logic to tell yourself there's no reason to be scared," she told herself. "You don't want to think anyone could come after you. That's the stuff of movies. Besides, you're here all alone, and the doors are locked. Nothing can happen. Oh!" She jumped when she heard the front door open.

It was supposed to be locked. Her heartbeat filled her ears as she peeked out the door, down the hallways, and into the lobby.

"Mom?" Annie walked in with all three dogs on their leashes. "Are you here?"

"Annie!" Stephanie rushed out. The dogs swirled at her feet, but she quickly moved past them to lock the door. "You were supposed to be in Portland."

"It didn't work out on such short notice," Annie explained, unclipping the dogs. "Jenna was sick, and Violet had to work. I figured I'd go ahead and come in, and that would save you from having to get these guys on your lunch break."

"You didn't have to do that," Stephanie protested, rubbing Sherlock's head as he leaned against her. "You still could've enjoyed a day off for yourself."

"Obviously, you must've needed me if you're keeping the door locked," Annie pointed out. "What's with that, anyway?"

Stephanie didn't like being dishonest with her daughter, but how could she possibly tell her the truth? Fortunately, she already had a story she'd been telling her clients all morning. "I heard some rumors about dangerous fugitives in the area, so I'm keeping the door locked no matter what. No walk-ins, and I'm sticking to my appointment list. I know it feels extreme, but I'd much rather be safe than sorry."

"Oh. I hadn't heard. Okay." Annie stepped forward to peek into the office.

"The fugitives aren't here if that's what you're worried about." Stephanie bent to pick up Jacques. He kept sending her images of being cuddled while he danced around on her feet, so she had no doubt about what he wanted.

Annie smiled. "No, I was just checking to see if your 'friend' Bennett is here again today."

"Don't you use finger quotes at me, young lady," Stephanie replied. "No, Bennett is out running errands today."

"You mean you didn't keep your big, strong man around to keep you safe from the bad guys lurking around town?" Annie batted her eyelashes and clasped her hands under her chin. Then she burst out laughing.

"You're full of it today," Stephanie noted with a smile. "I should put you in time out, but instead, I'll let you mop the floor in exam room three. A very excited young pit bull named Mr. Puddles decided to live up to his name. I cleaned up the worst of it, but it could use a deeper clean."

"Awesome. I'm so glad I came into work today."

Annie couldn't hold her deadpan face for long as she headed toward the supply closet for the mop bucket. "Anything else exciting happening around here?"

"No. It worked out that we weren't overbooked today, so it's been pretty slow." Stephanie headed into the office to get some paperwork done while they waited for the next appointment.

A short time later, when she was restocking the supplies that'd come in a couple of days ago, Annie rushed into the exam room. "Mom! I've just brought a man into the lobby with his dog."

Stephanie nearly dropped one of the bottles of lavender oil she was putting in the cabinet. She caught it against her shirt and put it safely away. "I'm not taking any walk-ins today. There's even a sign on the door that says so."

"I know, but his husky was hit by a car. He's all covered in blood, and we were the closest place. I put them in over in room three." Annie's forehead was creased with worry.

Stephanie's training and compassion took over. This could be a life-or-death situation, and she couldn't just turn them away. "You finish up with these supplies, then. I'll go see what I can do."

Her heart was racing as she jogged into the room. The scent of blood hit her nostrils and curdled her stomach. Stephanie's eyes first fell to the dog. His thick, gray fur was matted with blood. He held one paw up off the floor, and a pitiful whine emitted from his throat.

"Sir, this isn't a dog." Stephanie looked up at the older man who held the other end of the leash. Pockmarked scars dappled his cheeks beneath cold, hard eyes. "That's a wolf."

"He's only part wolf," he assured her in a smooth voice that didn't fit his image. "You don't have to worry about him. He needs your help."

Stephanie took another step into the room and looked at the dog once again. She'd very recently seen several wolves, and there was no doubt this was one of them. Her blood froze in her veins as images from its mind flickered across hers. Teeth flashing and tearing. Blood. Undertones of anger and violence flooded through her. This animal could have no idea she could pick up on such things, but those vicious thoughts hit her like a bullet.

If she needed any confirmation, Stephanie got it as soon as she looked back up at the man. Any worried caregiver would be watching his animal more than any veterinarian. They would probably also be hunched down on the floor, trying to help or at least soothe their pet. The guy continued to stare at Stephanie, and a hint of a smile curled his lips as the wolf lifted its head, locked its eyes with hers, and growled, baring its sharp fangs.

It was them.

Stephanie backed out of the room and slammed the door. She darted back into the exam room where she'd left Annie and flicked the lock. "Call 911."

"What the hell?" Cotton swabs spilled from Annie's hand as she grabbed for the phone on the wall. She dropped it and picked it up again. "What's happening?"

"That dog wasn't hit by a car, and they're not here for medical attention." Stephanie's mind felt like it was going to split in half. She couldn't possibly keep this secret much longer. She'd tried her best to keep Annie out of it, but the inevitable had happened. She understood now just how torn Bennett had felt about leaving her there that morning.

"Oh my god," Annie whispered, her hand shaking as she dialed. Her eyes widened. "Is it one of the fugitives?"

When she was little, Stephanie had always told Annie not to lie because those lies would come right back around to bite her. Now, she was experiencing that lesson for herself. The police wouldn't listen to anything Annie had to say if she started spouting off about fugitives because there weren't any. "I don't know. Just tell them we've got intruders."

"My name is Annie Caldwell. I'm at the Caldwell Naturopathic Veterinary Clinic on Barger. We've got an intruder." She paused as she listened to the operator. "I don't know. We're in a locked exam room, and he's trying to break down the door."

Stephanie watched the wooden door pulse inward with every pounding it received. Deep growls echoed from the small space beneath the door, making the hairs on the back of her neck stand up. She searched for something she could use to barricade it with. The exam table was an old one she'd bought secondhand, the kind that was on top of a solid wood cabinet. It was heavy enough to keep anyone out but also heavy enough that it couldn't be moved. The chair was on wheels and wouldn't do any good. There was no window since the back of the room shared a wall with the office area. She could hear Sherlock, Penelope, and Jacques going crazy. At least they seemed to be staying out of the way. "Tell them to hurry!"

"They've got someone on the way," Annie assured her. "They're staying on the line with me until—hello? Shit. The line is dead."

"Oh fuck." These guys knew what they were

doing. Stephanie had tried to tell herself that the peaceful, quiet morning had meant these guys had given up or weren't really after her at all. She'd been so wrong. A heavy sense of dread settled over her shoulders as a splinter of wood popped off the trim around the door. She touched her pocket, remembering that she needed to call Bennett. Her cell phone wasn't there. Where had she left it? "We've got to think, Annie. Is there anything in here we can defend ourselves with?"

Annie gestured helplessly at the cotton swabs now lying scattered on the table. "Not unless we can hit them with a tranquilizer, but I'd rather not get that close to them."

A heavy crack split the air as the door began to give. The metal knob was holding, but the wood around it was much more vulnerable. "We might not have a choice."

"Why don't they just leave?" Annie asked. "What could they possibly want from us?"

Stephanie's throat was dry. She'd sworn to Bennett that she would keep his secret, but she was quickly seeing that there was an expiration date on that promise. "They're not really after us, sweetheart. It's Bennett. They want him."

"What?" Annie asked shrilly. "I thought these were fugitives!"

"They probably aren't. Bennett is in an interesting line of work, and he's made some enemies along the way." Annie was already scared. Would it really do any good to push her past her senses with the news of shifters? Stephanie thought not. They might very well die there today if the police didn't come quickly enough. A new wave of guilt moved over her as she realized just what some poor officer was about to stumble into when he or she arrived. At least they'd have the advantage of a gun, but would that be enough? There were so many possibilities, and they were too hard to track. Her mind was firing off in all directions, but none led to the two of them getting out of there alive.

Annie's eyes were wide. A white line of strain showed around her mouth, and her forehead was in danger of a permanent crease. "This is insane!"

That wasn't even the half of it. "You're angry, and you've got every right to be. The police are on their way, and we'll have a very long talk once all this is over."

The door burst into two pieces, now dangling pitifully from its hinges as the bloody wolf and the man posing as his owner came in. He grinned when he saw the two women cowering in the back of the room. "What a pretty sight we have here. A two-for-one deal."

Stephanie moved in front of Annie. "Just let her go. She doesn't know about any of this and has no idea what's happening. She's just my worker."

"Oh, really?" He stepped closer, his fetid breath hitting Stephanie's face as he spoke. "Then why did I hear her call you Mom?"

She gritted her teeth, regretting every mistake she'd ever made. If she could at least get Annie out of this, then it would all be okay. Her vision darkened around the edges as fear threatened to shut her down completely. "I think you were mistaken."

His laugh was like sandpaper. "I don't think so." With a motion so quick she couldn't avoid it, his hand reached out and snagged her chin. He turned Stephanie's face from side to side, inspecting her with a frown. "So Bennett Westbrook has lowered himself to consorting with humans? Disgusting. He's always been a pain in the ass, but it turns out he's got bad taste, too."

Stephanie didn't care what this guy thought of her. She just wanted to live. Tears burned her eyes. "Let us go. We don't have anything to do with this."

"Oh, but you do. You might not understand it,

but Bennett will. I'd tell you to give him a message for me, but you won't live long enough to see him again." He laughed as he took a step backward.

That small amount of space he created between them didn't last long as he quickly changed shape. He fell to all fours, catching himself easily on wide paws and sturdy legs. His face stretched into a muzzle, turning his scratchy laugh into a low and menacing growl. Stephanie watched the transformation in horror. She'd already seen Bennett do this once but in the opposite direction. The man who'd stood before her a moment ago had no weapons on him that she'd been able to see. That was because his weapon had been inside him, just waiting to come out.

"What the fuck was that?!" Annie cried.

He charged. Stephanie dodged to the side, pushing Annie behind her. The exam room was small, with hardly any room to maneuver. These wolves were too fast and too strong. His teeth snapped an inch from her face. Stephanie knew he was only toying with her.

The bloody wolf went for Annie. She screamed as she fended him off with the wheeled stool, the only thing she'd been able to grab. He lunged again, his growl filling the room.

Stephanie's mind raced. She'd gone through tons of training about how to calm an aggressive or scared dog, but none of that would help her now. This wasn't just a dog there for an exam. This was a wolf who was hell-bent on killing her. Now that he was in his animal form, she had the same wave of psychic information she'd received from the other wolf. His yellow eyes bored into hers, and she knew he was still laughing at her.

In her peripheral vision, the bottle of sanitizing spray stood out. Stephanie grabbed it and pulled the trigger, aiming the liquid right at those yellow eyes. A horrible noise emanated from his throat as he thrashed, giving her just a moment of time. Stephanie moved backward around the exam table, grabbing Annie's arm on the way. They bolted out of the exam room, scrambling for their lives as the wolves came after them.

She'd had nightmares in which she couldn't run fast enough to get away from whatever was chasing her. Now, it felt like all those nightmares had come to life. The wolves were too fast and too determined. They wanted blood, and they were going to get it.

Annie screamed, a noise that sent a whole new bolt of terror through Stephanie's blood. Stephanie turned just in time to see the bloody wolf sink his teeth into her daughter's leg, just above her knee. The force of it sent her flying forward. Stephanie pulled hard on her arm, willing her to get back up and keep running. They had to keep going. They had to keep trying. She didn't want to die there.

The glass in the front door shattered, flying into the lobby. Stephanie's blood was heated, but the sound sent a chill up her spine. Were there more of them? Was this truly the end? No. No. It just couldn't be.

"Stephanie!"

She turned to see Bennett burst through the broken door. His eyes were dark with anger as he charged across the floor. His fangs descended as he headed for her, and she watched in dismay and relief as his wolf erupted from his body. He leaped past her, landing on top of the bloody wolf. They locked together, biting and clawing as they tumbled down the hallway.

Another wolf followed closely on his heels. Stephanie hardly had a chance to see the police officer in his human form before he raced after Bennett. It was only then that she realized how close her own pursuer had been to closing his teeth on the back of her arm.

Stephanie scrambled backward, pulling a terrified Annie after her. A river of blood streaked the floor. With the sound of the wolves fighting, her own screaming, and Annie's terrified whimpers, Stephanie felt like she was swimming through all the noise. Adrenaline and fear were fueling her now.

The back door slammed open, and the wolves continued their fighting outside. Stephanie turned around, wondering what would happen next, and realized she had no real way of knowing if any new arrivals were the enemy or not. The whole thing felt hopeless.

A moment later, Bennett came running through the back door in his human form, the police officer behind him. "They're gone for now, but we've got to get out of here."

"We can't right now." Stephanie clamped her hand down on Annie's leg. "I've got to get her stabilized. She's been bitten."

11

"There's a first aid kit on the wall just inside the office," Stephanie said. "She's bleeding badly, though."

The police officer who'd arrived with Bennett quickly came to her side as Bennett handed him the first aid kit. "Let me handle this," he said, his voice gentle but firm as he flipped the case open. "She needs your reassurance right now."

Stephanie had plenty of medical training, even if it was on animals instead of people, but she understood what he was doing. She let him take over on Annie's leg as she moved up toward her head. "It's all right, baby. We're going to get this taken care of."

"How bad is it?" Annie asked, her voice shaking.

She didn't want to tell her. "I'm not sure yet. I think you'll at least need some stitches, though."

"I'm so cold." Annie was sprawled on the floor, but she reached out for her mother's hand.

The three dogs, having realized the danger had passed, came out of the office. Sherlock and Penelope had their tails between their legs and heads down as they approached Annie, sniffing her and whining. Jacques, suddenly deciding he would've been able to fend off the vicious wolves himself, barked angrily as he skittered down the hallway.

"I know, sweetheart. It'll be okay. We'll get you patched up enough to get to the hospital, and you'll be fine."

Bennett walked back into the room, though Stephanie hadn't even realized he'd stepped away again. He'd grabbed the blanket from the office and knelt next to Stephanie as he draped it carefully over Annie. "This is Officer Kane Glenwood," he said softly as he put his hand on Stephanie's shoulder. "He's in my pack."

She looked at the dark-haired man who was busy staunching the blood that had already soaked through Annie's pant leg. "I'm glad you guys are here."

"Mom." Annie was sobbing. "I don't understand

what's going on right now. Did I really see all of that?"

"Yes." She swept a soothing hand over Annie's hair. "I know it doesn't make much sense, but I'll explain it all later. Right now, we just need to get you taken care of." She looked at Bennett. "Can you call an ambulance?"

He closed his eyes for a moment and shook his head. "We can't do that."

"What do you mean?" she fired off sharply. She'd already been through so much in a short amount of time, and this was the last thing she was expecting to hear. "She's bleeding. A stupid band-aid isn't going to fix that!"

"I know. Stephanie, she was bitten by a shifter." Bennett took her face in his hands and made sure she was looking him in the eye. "That means she's going to become one now. She's going to become one of us."

Her face twitched and spasmed as anger, confusion, and shock fought for space in her features. "What the fuck are you telling me right now? I thought you said you were born this way."

"Yes." His eyes were filled with sadness as he rubbed his thumbs across her cheekbones. "That's true, but it can happen this way, too. If someone is bitten, especially if the bite is deep, they become a shifter."

"Isn't there anything we can do about it?" Stephanie could hear the shrillness in her own voice.

"No." He swallowed. "It's going to happen. The first thing we have to do is get her taken care of medically, but we can't do that at a regular hospital. They don't know about us, and they don't know how we work. We've got to take her to the packhouse."

"But..." Stephanie tore away from Bennett to look down at her daughter. Her baby. She'd cleaned so many scrapes and cuts and burns. She'd held her and rocked her, and she'd been with her when she had to make tough decisions. Being a mother wasn't an easy job, but it was always one she'd been up for. She'd been happy to dive in with both feet and loved seeing Annie become an intelligent, beautiful young woman. Now, though, she had no idea how to help.

"We have healers there who can help her better than anyone at the hospital can," Kane said as he used medical tape to hold some gauze in place over the wound. "We have different methods, but that's what's needed. The threat of exposure is too great at the hospital."

"I just..." Everything inside her was fighting

against this. Her daughter was horribly injured, and they needed to get her some real medical care immediately. But Bennett's secret was now Annie's, though she was barely hanging onto consciousness and had no idea. Stephanie felt completely helpless. It was her job to help those in need, but she couldn't do anything right now. "Okay."

"We'll get her there in my squad car," Kane offered. "I'll have to leave after that, but Dawn and Joan can take care of her better than any of the rest of us can."

The next actions the men took happened so fast. Kane went out the front door and pulled his squad car around to the back so no one would see them load a bleeding woman inside. Bennett pulled one of the exam room doors off its hinges with a quick flick of the screwdriver from his Swiss Army knife and wedged it into place over the shattered glass door. "It's not perfect, but it'll have to do for the moment. I can get someone to come back and fix it."

"Don't worry about it." Stephanie's body had been flooded with fear and adrenaline, and now she just felt numb as they carefully braced Annie on a blanket between them and carried her to the back door. "I really don't care about any of this as long as she's all right."

Sherlock, Penelope, and Jacques all followed them out the door. Jacques led the way into the back of the squad car, hopping right up into the back seat.

"We can't bring you guys." Stephanie wondered if her psychic connection to the dogs went both ways. The dogs didn't speak English, but could she tell them they'd have to stay there and wait for her.

"Just let them pile on in," Bennett suggested as he watched Penelope attempt to sit in Kane's lap. "They're pretty determined, and they'll be welcome at the packhouse."

As she squeezed into the backseat with Annie's head on her lap, Stephanie hoped *she* would be. Sherlock was warm on her feet as he settled into the floorboard, his head propped on Stephanie's knee so he could keep an eye on Annie. Since Kane couldn't drive with a pit bull on his lap, Penelope had to settle for sitting near Bennett. Jacques was everywhere, watching through the windows and staying alert. Images of the wolves from his perspective rushed through Stephanie's mind. They were massive monsters that towered over the little chihuahua, capable of snapping his head off with one bite.

Stephanie didn't feel she had much more advantage than the tiny dog.

Bennett was in the front passenger seat, but he

turned around and reached for her hand as the squad car rushed through traffic. "Stephanie, I'm so sorry. This never would've happened if I hadn't left. I should've been there. I should've come back sooner."

She was sick with worry, and the waves of nausea were coming closer together now as she felt Annie's pulse getting weaker. It felt like she should be angry, but Stephanie knew she had no real cause to be. "I was the one who insisted you drop me off this morning," she reminded him softly, wishing she could erase that sad look from his eyes.

"But I was the one who agreed to it. Every part of me told me not to do it. I should've figured out a different way." His hand clung even more tightly to hers.

"It's not your fault, Bennett. It's mine. I should've closed up and gone to the packhouse with you like you'd asked." If only, if only, if only. There weren't many decisions Stephanie regretted as a mother, but right now, she had a big one.

"She's going to be very well taken care of, Stephanie. I promise."

Stephanie pulled her eyes away from Annie and looked up at Bennett. He was her high school sweetheart. According to what he'd told her, he was her mate. It was a strange term, one she'd never thought to use for a lover. Right now, though, as she felt a deep sense of connection and trust with him, it felt right. Bennett meant every word he said, and she knew it.

That didn't mean she didn't have questions, which felt like a constant in her life at the moment. "Will I be able to stay with her? Or will I have to leave?" she asked quietly.

Another swell of pain moved across his face. "You can stay," Bennett said. "No one is going to question that. I never should have."

The drive felt like an eternity, though it was really only a few minutes. Kane had been in contact with someone ahead of time, and as they headed up the long driveway, Stephanie saw a garage door open. Several women and a couple of men met them in the garage as they pulled inside.

"I've got her feet. Hayden, can you get her arms?"

"No problem." A brawny man wearing a Eugene-Springfield Fire t-shirt moved Annie off Stephanie's lap with remarkable ease. He and a blonde man maneuvered Annie through a door and into the house. The dogs all came along as escorts, not even asking for permission.

A woman with long gray hair and beads around

her neck pointed her finger. "I've got the dining table cleared off. Put her there, please."

"I'm getting the last few things from the altar room," shouted a woman about Stephanie's age with butterscotch brown hair before she disappeared down the hall.

A teen girl peered around the corner and grinned when she saw the dogs. "Come here, puppies! You can come in the kitchen with me! Good dogs, I'll get you some treats!"

Several blankets and a pillow had been spread out on the dining table, turning it into a makeshift operating table. A woman in scrubs stood next to it. She was geared up with gloves and had a tray laid out with several instruments. As soon as Annie was on the table, she was peeling back the gauze and evaluating the wound. "I need to get some stitches in her right away to stop the bleeding."

The woman with gray hair sat down at the end of the table, right near Annie's head. "Annie, my name is Joan. We're going to take care of you. I just want you to stay with me, okay?" She put her hands on Annie's shoulders, took a deep breath, and closed her eyes.

The woman with the butterscotch hair came back, laying out several crystals and herbs on the table on the opposite side of the medical woman's instruments. Then she quickly turned to Stephanie and took her by the shoulders, her brown eyes gazing into hers. "Hi, my name's Lori. Are you injured, too?"

"No." She could barely hold her bile back. "I just want her to be okay."

"We're going to do everything we can, and that's more than it might seem. Some of it will look very strange, but I expect you've seen a lot of that today."

An ironic laugh escaped Stephanie's throat as a tear trickled down her cheek. "Like you wouldn't believe."

Lori smiled. "Trust me, I would. Why don't you have a seat right here. Brody, get her some water."

"Sure thing." The blonde man who'd helped carry Annie in headed off.

Bennett came to sit beside her as Brody handed her a glass of water. "Are you sure you want to stay in here? I can easily find a spot for you to lie down."

"No." Stephanie felt like absolute shit, and she was barely staying upright in the chair, but she couldn't leave Annie. "I need to be here."

Another man entered the room. "How's she doing, Dawn?"

"Stephanie, this is Rex. Our Alpha." Bennett

made the introduction, and some tension simmered in the air between them.

Rex reached out a hand. "It's nice to meet you, although I wish the circumstances were different."

There were so many new faces, several resembling each other. Stephanie knew she'd never get them straight, but it didn't matter right now.

"She's lost a lot of blood." Dawn, the woman in scrubs cleaning Annie's wound, replied. "I'll have a better idea of just what I'm dealing with once I'm done with this. If she could shift, she'd heal up in no time. That's not something we can teach her right now, so we'll have to rely on other methods."

Shift? Stephanie reeled all over again. Her daughter was no longer going to be human. It was impossible to comprehend. Bennett had told her that shifters could heal quickly, but Annie didn't know how to do that yet. It was so unfair.

Stephanie blinked and leaned her head on Bennett's shoulder. "I think I'm hallucinating. Her hands are green." She couldn't take her eyes away from Dawn, whose palms and fingers exuded an emerald halo as she worked.

"You're not hallucinating," Bennett replied softly. "Those are her healing powers. Some of the women in this family are witches as well as shifters. What you're seeing here is actually the best medical team Annie could possibly have right now."

It was then that Stephanie realized the older woman's hands were glowing as well. Lori had gone to sit next to her. She'd put her hands on Annie's back as well. She'd closed her eyes and tipped her head back. "Selene, we pray for your help. Our sister has so newly come to us and doesn't yet know the way. Halt time as only you know how, and give her the grace to come into herself and heal properly."

There were so many things happening in front of her that she didn't quite understand, but Stephanie was watching with pure fascination. The shifters worked in such perfect coordination, more like a trained team than a family. They'd instantly responded to a drastic situation, with everyone helping in whatever way they could. They were there for each other, and they were there for Annie.

Stephanie's healing methods weren't exactly traditional, but the lengths these women were going to stepped even beyond the bounds of her naturopathic training. Healing powers. Praying to someone named Selene. The warm glow they spread through Annie's body. It was incredible. She just had to hope it worked.

Dawn put fresh gauze over the wound and

checked Annie's vitals. "That's about all we can do right now. She needs to rest, and then we'll reevaluate her."

"You need some rest, too," Bennett said, rising from his seat.

"I want to stay here with her." Stephanie couldn't leave her alone, not after this.

"He's right." Dawn gave her a stern look. "You won't be any good to her if you're exhausted. Rest, and we'll make sure someone is with her constantly."

Stephanie didn't know Dawn at all beyond her name and her remarkable ability, but she recognized the authority of another medical professional. She nodded. "All right."

Bennett kissed the back of her hand. "Come on. Lori is already getting a room set up for you."

12

"Bennett, honey. I came as soon as I heard you were here, but I wasn't sure what was going on."

"Mom." Bennett rose from his seat in the living room. "What are you doing here?"

"Well, what's a mother supposed to do?" She rubbed her hands on his arms and checked him over for injuries. "I get a phone call from Kane saying the Bloodmoon Crew has been after you, and things are bad enough that you've had to take shelter at the packhouse. I'm not just going to sit at home and knit a pair of socks."

"You don't knit, Mom," he reminded her with a smile.

She patted his cheek. "No, but even if I did, it

wouldn't help right now. Talk to me. Tell me what's happening."

Bennett glanced over his shoulder toward the dining room. He could see that Brody's mate, Robin, had been stationed with Annie for the moment. The other women who'd worked with her had gone to rest, knowing they'd be needed later. Delicious scents were filtering in from the kitchen, so as usual, someone had taken up the role of making sure everyone was fed no matter what was happening. The beta's daughter, Ava, had kept the dogs entertained during the most crucial moments, but now they were all asleep under the dining table, waiting for Annie to wake up. "It's a little complicated."

She smiled at him. "Bennie, I'm a mom. I know how to do complicated."

If things were different, he would've asked her not to call him that. Bennett had outgrown that old nickname a long time ago, but it seemed trivial right now. "Let's go outside."

"Are you sure it's safe?" she asked as they stepped onto the front porch. The roof overhang protected them from the slow drizzle that'd started up. "My heart about flew out of my chest when Kane mentioned the Bloodmoon Crew."

"Rex has guards posted all around the perimeter

of the territory." Bennett moved over to a glider set up in front of the large picture window. "I'll have to remember to thank Kane personally for getting you involved."

Patricia sat down next to him and patted his knee. "Now, don't you be too upset with him. He's always seen you as a brother, and he sounded genuinely worried over the phone."

"No, I'm not." As Bennett watched the mist settle down on the driveway and pool into little glistening pearls on the porch railing, he realized he actually did need to thank Kane. If Nelson had ordered his men to come after Stephanie, his mom could likely be next. "It's much safer that you're here, actually, and you'll probably need to stay here for a while."

She gave him a look. "Bennett, you're going to have to tell me what's going on. All this waiting means I'm either going to have to start pacing or get a stiff drink. Or maybe both."

Both might be in order by the time he got through it all. Bennett knew she wasn't going to like what he had to say. "First of all, I've been contracted to take out the Bloodmoon Crew."

She clasped her hands and held them tightly against her stomach, something she'd always done when she was upset. "I had a terrible feeling it was something like that."

Bennett knew there was no better time to be honest, both with himself and with her. He'd tried to justify his actions to Rex earlier that morning. The meeting felt like it was a week ago now, and so much had changed. "It was only a matter of time before someone decided they didn't want to put up with them anymore. A Silvergrove came to me under the utmost confidentiality. The paycheck is a big one, but it wasn't about that for me. I'd been waiting for an excuse to wipe them off the face of the planet."

"I'm surprised Rex let you go after them, considering all the pack politics involved."

"I guess everyone was thinking about that besides me," Bennett chuckled. "I didn't give two shits about pacts or contracts or truces. I don't care that the Glenwoods had already repaid them for what they'd done. *I* hadn't repaid them. *I* hadn't had my revenge yet." As he spoke of it, Bennett could feel his blood boiling all over again. "The problem—one of many —is that they've grown stronger. I can't do it alone."

"I see." She stretched out the last word, knowing there had to be more and inviting him to continue.

She knew him well. He had to give her credit for

that. Bennett would never just run and hide at the packhouse. "Mom, do you remember Stephanie Caldwell?"

"What?" She turned on the glider's cushion to look at him fully. "Of course."

"She's here, Mom. We've found each other again. Unfortunately, that means the Bloodmoon Crew is after her as well. One of them bit her daughter, Annie. We had to bring her here, and now we're all just waiting to see what happens." He spoke quickly, wanting to get it all out before she could protest or ask too many questions and get him off track. "I know you and Dad didn't approve of her, but Stephanie is my mate. Time hasn't changed anything between us."

Her shoulders sagged, and she sat back against the glider. "Oh, Bennett."

"I know that's a lot to dump on you all at once, but you need to know the whole picture." His throat was tight.

"Oh, my goodness." She pressed two fingers to her forehead.

He waited for the inevitable explosion. As much as she must hate hearing any news about the Bloodmoon Crew, this had to be just as devastating for her.

The only difference was that she'd just have to deal with it this time.

"That poor, poor woman." Patricia pressed her fingers to her mouth now. "Having to witness her daughter being injured like that. And then, of course...we know what the outcome must be. Oh, I just can't even imagine. Oh, my."

Bennett watched her carefully, wondering if he was hearing her correctly. "I thought you'd be angry."

"Oh, I'm angry, all right." She took several short inhales as she tried to control her emotions, though her eyes were just as wet as everything else around them right now. "Just not for the reasons you might think."

He sat forward, firmly putting his feet on the porch so the glider couldn't move. "I think it's your turn to explain because I'm lost."

"Of course you are, darling. Of course you are, and it's all my fault." She puffed her cheeks as she let out a breath and looked toward the cloudy sky. Then she turned to him and took his hand. "This is one of those things that just feels impossible to let out."

"Take your time." Bennett said that, though he was feeling impatient. He didn't understand.

She let out another long sigh. "First of all, I truly

am sorry for Stephanie having to endure that. It's not easy, as a parent, to see your child struggle through anything. Medical, mental, emotional. It's all difficult. You want to fix everything for them, and even when there are some things you can fix, you can't just change the whole world to suit their needs. I just feel terribly sorry for her."

"That's nice of you." So his mother could relate to Stephanie on the level of being a mom. That much, at least, wasn't out of his realm of understanding.

"Sometimes," she continued, her voice catching in her throat, "when you think you're fixing things, you're actually making them worse. I've wondered many times what I might've done differently as your mother that would've given you a happy life because I know you've been miserable."

He wanted to deny that so he could take her pain away, but it was true.

"I don't think you would've gone into this line of work if you weren't still carrying around that deep sadness. I worry about you. I know you're a very talented man. With your natural skill and the training you received on the police force, you're good at what you do, even if I'd rather you be safely behind a desk for eight hours a day. That doesn't mean I'm not proud of you, though. You've found something that suits you, that you're good at, and that brings you a certain sense of satisfaction at the end of the day. Not everyone can say that, even when they're the CEO of a big company." She gave him a sad smile and squeezed his knee again.

He patted the back of her hand. "That's funny because I always figured I was nothing but a disappointment to you."

"No. No, Bennie. *I'm* the disappointment. I'm the only one who's done anything wrong." Tears slipped off her cheeks and fell onto the sleeve of her jacket.

"What do you mean?" He took her hand between both of his now. When was the last time he'd seen her cry? It'd probably been at his father's funeral, which was a long time ago now. Between his death and Rosa's, she'd probably cried many times since then, but never in front of him. She was always trying to be so strong, insisting she was fine and he needed to get back to work and not worry about her. "You were always a good mom."

"Sure, in many of the ways that people count," she agreed. "I took care of you when you were sick, and I made sure you actually understood your homework when I helped you with it. I encouraged you, and I wanted all the best things for you. But the biggest mistake I ever made was in agreeing with your father that you shouldn't date Stephanie any longer."

Bennett took a moment to absorb this, reliving some of those conversations from long ago in his head. His mother had been much younger then. Her hair had been more black than gray, the opposite of what it was now. She'd had fewer lines and fewer worries, but she'd been just as passionate as his father when she'd put her foot down about Stephanie. "I thought that was what you wanted."

"Maybe in the moment I thought I did," she admitted. "I didn't think much of it until your father started in. He was at that restaurant all the time, and he saw the whole thing unfold between the two of you. I thought he was just irritated because you were getting distracted from your work, and the restaurant meant a lot to him. When things started to get serious between you, he started up about her being human. Your father loved you so much, Bennett, and his concerns only ever came out of that. He looked at a future for you and a human woman and only saw how difficult it would be. Would the other shifters accept her? Could the two of you truly find any common ground when you were so different? And what about any children you might have? Would they be shifters or humans, and how would you each feel about it? He didn't think you could ever be happy."

"But she's my mate," Bennett said softly. "Human or not, there's a connection there that I can't deny. I felt that way even then."

"You were just a kid," she said with a smile. "That's what adults always tell themselves when they don't like the way a teenager thinks. They're just kids. It's a phase. They don't really know what they want, and they don't understand the world. I, too, wanted the best for you, so I went along with the whole thing. We knew you were far too stubborn to just do as we asked, not in this situation, so we demanded it."

"I had no idea," he said gruffly, thinking about all the years he could've had with Stephanie, years forever lost to time now. "I thought you hated her because she was human."

Patricia brushed away her tears, but they only continued to fall. "To be honest with you, I thought she was a very nice girl. She was pretty, of course, but she was so smart and energetic. She had big dreams, and I really didn't know what else I could want for my son. I should've known better, but we never really understand some things until we get a chance to look back on them."

"That's definitely true. I've been thinking about my own mistakes a lot. No offense, but I shouldn't have listened to you, Mom. I don't mean this in a disrespectful way, but I should've told you I'd never break up with Stephanie because I was fated to be with her. Hell, maybe I should've even kept seeing her behind your back. But you're right. It's a lot easier to look back and see what you should've done."

"I do hope you can forgive me, Bennett. I did my best, and I was trying so hard to make everyone happy. Your father, too. I think if he had the chance to see you the way I have, to see just how discontented you've been with your life, he'd be sitting right here saying the same things I am."

He looked at her once again, really trying to see her as a person and not just a mother. It was impossible to distinguish the two, but parents made mistakes. It was what they did with those mistakes that truly mattered. "Of course I do, Mom."

"Thank you, honey. Truly. I've lived with that for a long time. I know that fate doesn't always give us what we imagine. Sometimes, it doesn't even give us what we want. I sure wouldn't have asked for a man who always left his socks on the floor the way your father did!"

They laughed together for a moment, each reflecting on the losses they'd suffered when he and Rosa had died.

She nodded toward the front door of the pack-house. "Does all this mean that you and Stephanie are back together?"

Bennett also looked at the front door. Stephanie was in there. Her daughter, whose life and future still hung in the balance, was also in there. "If you had asked me this morning, I would've thought I knew the answer. Finding Stephanie again was like a miracle, like fate had decided to give us a second chance. But that was before the Bloodmoon Crew attacked. If you want to talk about mistakes, I have plenty to atone for. I don't know if she'll be willing to forgive me, and I can't even ask her. Not while we're still waiting to see what happens with Annie, and maybe not ever."

"Mm, yes. That's certainly difficult. Would you like advice from a silly old woman who's still figuring things out?" She raised her brows at him hopefully.

"Of course, I would."

"Don't think about any of that right now." She

pointed to the door. "Go in there and be there for her. Comfort her, and make sure she has everything she needs. Do whatever you can to help Annie and to keep both of them safe. This isn't the time for deciding futures and discussing relationships. It can all wait until later. Your only job right now is to be the good man I know you are. Think you can handle that?"

In a way, he didn't. Bennett wanted Stephanie to be a part of his life, but they hadn't really talked it over or discussed what it would mean for the two of them. They'd been thrown together in their efforts to survive, and of course, they'd fallen into bed together, but that had been the extent of it. His mother was right. This wasn't the time to figure out all the details of the future. That would have to come later. "Yeah. I think I can."

13

THE KNOCK ON THE DOOR WAS GENTLE, BUT IT startled Stephanie straight out of a deep sleep. She bolted upright in the bed, and it only took her a moment to remember exactly where she was. "Hm? Is Annie okay?"

Lori peered into the room, her face kind and gentle. "Everything is fine. I brought you a change of clothes and some food. You needed some rest, but I think this other stuff is pretty essential, too."

"Oh. Thank you." Stephanie looked down, realizing her clothes were caked and stiff with blood. She'd been so focused on Annie that she hadn't even noticed. Her stomach growled as soon as she glanced at the bowl of bean and sausage stew and the warm roll beside it.

"You're more than welcome to take a shower." Lori nodded toward the attached bathroom. "We keep everything stocked with towels and other amenities, so it's ready whenever you want to use it."

Stephanie took the tray Lori offered and perched it on her lap. The stew smelled absolutely delicious. "Is Annie awake yet?"

"No, but she's doing well," Lori assured her quickly. "Dawn just went and checked on her a few minutes ago. I didn't get much of a chance to explain before, but she's the pack healer and a very skilled nurse. She's our secret weapon when it comes to injuries around here."

"It was remarkable watching the three of you work together." Stephanie could've easily written it off as some wild dream if she wasn't there in the Glenwood packhouse, discussing it with the kind female leader of these wolves. "I'm so grateful for everything you've done for her."

"No thanks are necessary, but we're not done." Lori sat in the armchair near the window, studying Stephanie's face as she spoke. "Bennett told you she's going to become one of us, right? A shifter?"

The stew was excellent, but Stephanie suddenly had a hard time swallowing. She'd been more concerned with making sure Annie stayed alive than anything else, and she hadn't even allowed herself to fully process the rest of it yet. "Yes."

"I know that's hard to understand. I can sympathize because I believed I was just a normal human for most of my life," Lori replied. "Annie isn't obligated to stay here, but we want to help her as much as we can. She's going to have to learn how to live her new life, and it wouldn't be right to make her do that on her own. If we can show her how to shift, she'll not only heal faster but have a better understanding of who she is now."

Stephanie poked her spoon into her bowl. "So she'll turn into a wolf."

"Yes. It may take some time, but she's young. I'm sure she'll do well, and then she'll start feeling much better."

"I don't even know how to explain this to her," Stephanie replied, feeling sadness and grief wash through her. "I'm still trying to figure it all out myself."

"That's why we're here, and that's why *she's* here. She won't go through this alone. There's plenty more stew in the kitchen, by the way. I can get you another bowl if you'd like."

"No, that's all right." She'd polished it off quickly and reached for the roll. "I feel awkward asking you this, but what should I be doing while all this happens with Annie?"

Lori smiled again. She had a motherly way about her, though she couldn't have been much older than Stephanie. "You can be right there with us if you want."

"Really?"

"She's your daughter." Lori stood and flicked the hem of her shirt. "She's going to need you. Take care of yourself and get freshened up. Come on out when you're ready. Nothing will happen until you're there." With yet another sweet smile, Lori left the room.

Sticking the roll in her mouth, Stephanie set the tray on the dresser and headed into the bathroom. Desperate to return to her daughter, she hardly wanted to take the time to shower until she saw herself in the mirror. Her clothes were crusted with blood, and several smears of it had dried on her face and neck. Loops of hair had worked their way loose from her braid, and she looked like hell. The spacious walk-in shower was calling to her.

She washed away as much of the terror and trauma of the day as she could, thrilled to find a large pump bottle of citrus body lotion on the counter and several face products in the cabinet. Only when you found yourself in dire situations did you truly appreciate the smallest things in life, like hot water and a fluffy towel. Lori had guessed her size well. As soon as she was dressed and her hair was again tamed into a damp braid, Stephanie peered into the hallway.

Her room was only a short walk down the hall from the dining-turned-operating room. She found Annie still on the table, asleep but with some of the color returned to her face. Lori, Dawn, and Joan were all there again, and a couple of other women had joined them.

"Stephanie." Lori came to her side as soon as she saw her. "I'd like you to meet Angela and Robin. We asked them to come in and help because they can understand Annie's situation better than anyone."

Robin, a curvy woman with strawberry blonde hair that just reached her jawline, took Stephanie's hand. "It's so nice to meet you. I know the circumstances are odd, and I can't say this is how I would normally introduce myself, but I used to be human."

"Same here," Angela said with a little wave. "It's a lot to take in when it's happening, but it's going to be okay."

"Is it?" Stephanie stepped up to her daughter's side, carefully brushing a strand of hair from Annie's face.

Dawn nodded. "Yes. I have every confidence in that. She'll be doing great once we get her through this first shift."

"Where's Bennett?"

"He had some other things to take care of, and I told him to shoo," Lori replied. "I don't know your daughter, but it can be a bit awkward and embarrassing when you're learning how to be who you are. We all decided that, since the circumstances allowed, it would be best if she was just with other women for now."

Stephanie nodded, surprised at how good it felt to be there amongst people who were so considerate of one another. They didn't even know Annie, yet they rallied around her as one of their own. Stephanie supposed her daughter technically was now, but it still touched her to know these women were so eager to help. Stephanie had worried she might not be allowed to stay since she was a human, but they'd gone out of their way to make her feel comfortable and welcome. She even felt safe.

Did that mean Bennett's parents had had something against her personally?

"Mom?" Annie stirred, her breathing awkward and her brow wrinkling. "Is that you?"

"I'm right here, baby. You're all fixed up now.

You're going to be okay." Her heart lifted at hearing her daughter's voice, but her stomach dropped. She knew there was still a lot to go over. "Bennett brought you to some people who knew how to help."

"But the wolves," Annie insisted, her voice tired and cracking. "Was that real?"

"Yes, honey."

Annie pulled in a deep breath and winced. "It hurts."

"Where do you hurt, dear?" Dawn asked.

"Everywhere."

"Probably bumps and bruises," Dawn replied. "I didn't find any evidence of other major damage."

Stephanie wondered how she would know, but there was much she didn't understand when it came to Dawn's mystical talents. "There's a lot we have to tell you, sweetie. Some of it won't really make sense."

Annie blinked and pressed her hand to her forehead. She stretched and then stopped, her eyes wide. "My leg fucking kills!"

"A wolf bite will do that to you," Dawn replied calmly. "Let's get you into the living room. Right now, I think the couch will be more comfortable than this table. There you go. Just put your arm around me like that, but don't try to put any weight on your right leg. I've got you. Good job."

Stephanie walked on the other side of Annie as they escorted her to a better spot. The dogs had reappeared from the kitchen now that Annie was awake, and they followed along to complete her entourage. Penelope and Sherlock were content enough to settle in at her feet, but Jacques always had his own ideas. He hopped in her lap and curled into a tiny ball, his big brown eyes peeking out from the shelter of his skinny tail and watching the room.

Annie stroked his back and gave her mom a troubled look. "I think I might be crazy, Mom."

She knew that feeling very well. "Because of some of the things you've seen?"

"Sort of, but also because I believe them. I don't know how to explain it, really. I mean, I think I saw a dude turn into a wolf. Then I remember you said something about Bennett being like that. It has to be some sort of delusion, but it actually sort of makes sense. So, yeah. I think I'm crazy."

"I think we can help you understand." Lori sat in a chair nearby and began to explain.

Stephanie listened in fascination as each of the women took turns, patiently talking about their own pasts and experiences and answering all of Annie's questions. Dawn had been born like this, just like her mother, Joan. They carried a responsibility toward their pack that they took very seriously. Lori, as she'd already briefly mentioned to Stephanie, had believed she was just a normal human being until she'd met her mate, Rex. Her entire life had changed, but only for the better. Robin's transformation had been an accident, but it had brought her into the happiest time of her life. Angela recounted how she'd been changed to save her life, which seemed particularly relevant to Annie's case.

"That's where we come back to you, my dear," Joan said as she ran her fingers along a strand of purple beads around her neck. "If you'd had the knowledge and capability to shift right away, you wouldn't have needed our healing powers and perhaps not even stitches. You're recovering well, and even that is due to the wolf that now lives inside of you. Can you feel it? Almost like another voice or another consciousness inside you?"

Annie had been holding Stephanie's hand as they listened, and now her grip tightened. She stared down at her lap for a moment before she looked up at Joan. "As much as I can't believe I'm saying this, yes."

Joan gave her an approving nod. "Good. That's a great start."

"We'd like to help you learn to shift. I know it

seems very soon, but it's the best way we can help ensure you heal. Could I get you some food first, though?" Lori asked.

Annie pressed her free hand to her stomach. "I don't think I could handle any food right now. Thank you."

"No problem. We have plenty whenever you're ready. We should move these sweet dogs back to the kitchen. This might freak them out a little." Lori stepped to the door and clicked her tongue.

Stephanie prepared herself to help wrangle them, but it was quickly apparent that her help wasn't needed. The dogs responded to Lori the same way they had to Bennett. Stephanie picked up vague signals from them and understood that they saw the shifters as leaders, like big dogs but with special powers and authority.

Dawn leaned forward. "Do you think you're ready to try?"

"I'll do my best," Annie said with a shrug. "I'm not going to say I don't believe all of you, but I'm still not sure I really will unless it actually happens."

Robin laughed. "That sounds pretty reasonable to me! We're going to start by getting you in touch with your inner wolf. You said you can feel it, so right now, you need to really pay attention to it.

Close your eyes and explore it. Let it expand within you and be itself. Don't try to hold it back."

"Most humans are raised to keep their emotions in check and hide the parts of themselves that they don't want the rest of the world to see," Angela added. "It's hard, but you have to change the way you think about that."

"Now we need to work on some breathing techniques." Joan had the same maternal vibe as Lori, and her voice was soothing.

Annie, still with her eyes closed, smiled. "At least that's something I'm familiar with." She squeezed Stephanie's hand again.

In some ways, Stephanie had worried she was losing her daughter. Annie had grown up so fast, and even though she was proud to see the brilliant young woman she'd become, it was hard. At least some element of her time with Stephanie was still relevant to her new life as a shifter. Stephanie had guided her through calming and meditative breaths many times.

Lori had returned from the kitchen. "When you breathe in, envision your wolf strengthening and growing larger inside you. When you breathe out, imagine that your wolf comes right out of your lungs and into the room."

Annie did as she was told, her chest rising and falling, but she still looked entirely human.

"Be patient with yourself," Robin advised. "Relax as much as possible and know it will happen in its time."

It was so hard to watch. Stephanie knew this needed to happen, but she wished she knew more about how to help. Annie would need to learn how to work this new part of her life, and she was fortunate enough that she had all the right people around to help her with it. The Glenwood women were so gracious and kind.

Annie let her breath out through her mouth, and a line of thick fur erupted on her arm. She jerked her head upright, her eyes snapping open, and let out a yelp of surprise when she saw it. With a shaking hand, she reached over and touched it. "Holy shit."

"That's wonderful," Joan encouraged. "Great job."

"It shows you're doing everything right," Robin added. "Just keep at it!"

"Okay." Annie nodded. She closed her eyes again and worked on her breathing. She relaxed into the couch as she took several more breaths, but nothing happened.

Then Annie's body jerked forward. She nearly fell off the couch, but Dawn caught her by the shoulders. Annie spasmed, several gasps and strange noises escaping her throat as her new inner wolf took over. Wolf ears poked up through her hair as it retracted into fur. The entire shape of her body completely transformed. It was only a matter of a few seconds, but Stephanie watched in fascination and horror as her daughter became a wolf.

"Perfect!" Joan exclaimed, clapping her hands. "You're beautiful, dear!"

"It's going to feel strange for a while, but medically, you're probably going to feel much better," came Dawn's clinical assertion.

"Once we know it's safe, we'll take you out in the woods so you can *really* feel what it's like." Robin smiled and clasped her hands together. "It's absolutely amazing."

Angela laughed. "You'll definitely need that training, and don't feel ashamed about it. I looked like a baby deer when it first happened to me. But you'll get the hang of it."

Stephanie dared to reach over and set her hand down on Annie's new pelt. It was thick and warm and very real against her palm. *Oh, my sweet baby girl.*

I'm okay.

Every muscle in Stephanie's body tensed. She'd heard that. She knew she'd really heard that, and it hadn't come out of Annie's mouth. *Can you hear me?*

If a wolf could smile—something Stephanie wasn't really sure about at this point—Annie was definitely smiling at her. *Clear as a bell. You always said you were an animal psychic. I can tell you for sure now that you are.*

"Quiet ladies," Joan said in a hushed tone to the other women, who were going on about all they'd learned and all the mistakes they'd made along the way. "I think something special is happening here."

Oh, my god. Tears blurred Stephanie's vision, and she blinked them away quickly. She didn't want to miss a single second of this. *This is amazing. I thought I was losing you, Annie.*

No way, Mom. I'm tougher than that.

I know. Stephanie put her arms around the beautiful wolf's neck and held her close. *I love you so much.*

14

"Have you seen anything?" Bennett caught Hayden as he was coming in from his shift. The number of guards had grown since he'd arrived at the Glenwood packhouse with Stephanie and Annie, and Rex had called for all hands on deck. Anyone available was to report for duty, and the most vulnerable of their pack had either been brought to the packhouse or at least checked in on. That should've made Bennett feel better, but it didn't.

Hayden shook his head as he shrugged out of his jacket. "Nothing but branches blowing in the breeze. That should be a good thing, but the look on your face suggests I should be sorry I didn't see anything."

Bennett let out an irritated huff. "You're right. It

should be good. I'm just eager to get my hands on those assholes."

"I'm sure you'll get your chance," Hayden replied, glancing back out the doorway he'd just come through. "I don't know as much about the Bloodmoon Crew as you, but I know they're not ones to give up."

"Right." That was exactly what Bennett wanted because he wouldn't give up, either. It was also terrifying since Nelson and his wolves were now after Annie and Stephanie. They'd run into an unexpected surprise at the animal clinic, but small defeats weren't enough to make them lose the war.

Hayden put a hand on his shoulder. "We'll get it figured out, Cuz. We always do. In the meantime, I'm heading up to the kitchen to see what's cooking. I heard Sarah made that awesome stew, and Tiffany sent over a few things from the café. It'll be way better than anything I attempt to cook at home or what we have at the firehouse. Want to come with?"

"No, thanks." Bennett had eaten what little he could manage to choke down. The food was excellent, of course. Someone always stepped up to create something delicious and homemade in a crisis, and Bennett was typically a believer in taking care of yourself no matter what else was happening. This wasn't the same as being pursued by a murderous crew looking to take him out. It was far bigger, big enough that food wouldn't help.

"Bennett." Kane stepped into the basement meeting room. He'd changed out of his uniform and brought the scent of stew with him down from the kitchen. "I can hear you pacing from upstairs."

"Wouldn't you be?" Bennett snapped. "I feel like a caged animal. First, Rex gives me the Alpha command and prevents me from doing anything to take out those pricks. Then they come after my mate and her daughter, and you know how the hell that went. I can't even help with that, though. Lori kicked me out of the dining and living room while they figured out how things were going with Annie."

Kane shook his head. "If there's anything I know about women, you'd better let them do whatever they're doing and stay out of it."

"But it's my fault," Bennett insisted.

"You can go around pointing the finger all day. But even if that finger is pointing right back at you, the most important thing is that the situation is handled. Annie is in a vulnerable position right now. No offense, but she doesn't need some detective-turned-vigilante at the moment. She needs exactly what she's got up there: her mother and the other women in this pack. I know you don't like that, but it's true." Kane stepped over to the long bank of windows and looked out.

He was right. Bennett knew that. He still didn't like it. "I shouldn't have let Stephanie stay at her clinic, but I did anyway. Maybe I can't help Annie right now, but I need to do something, damn it! Rex won't even let me take a shift on guard duty."

"Can you blame him?" Kane's blue eyes were calm and reasonable, which only irritated Bennett more. "This might be our pack, but it's not entirely unlike the force. Letting someone work on a case that's too close to them is a liability."

Bennett hunched his shoulders. "I was going to thank you for your help this morning, but now I'm not so inclined." Why did he have to be right when Bennett was so eager to argue?

Kane laughed. "I'll just let you thank me double later."

"For what?" Bennett narrowed his eyes.

"I was going to suggest that the two of us get our asses up into Rex's den and talk about exactly what's going on here. I know I hesitated before because I didn't want to ruffle feathers. After what I saw this morning, I'm more than happy to back you up." He grinned. "You know, just like the good old days."

Bennett smacked him on the arm and headed for the stairs. "The coffee's much better here, though."

As he emerged on the main floor of the pack-house, his wolf surged inside him. It knew Stephanie was there, just on the other side of the wall. Whether Lori and the other women thought so or not, his mate needed him. She shouldn't have to go through any of this alone. Their relationship was up in the air, yes. There was no telling if Stephanie would still want anything to do with him now that her daughter was no longer human. That didn't stop him from wanting to be right there next to her during the entire process. He clenched his jaw and headed straight down the hall to Rex's den.

They found him standing in front of the window, his hands clasped behind his back as he looked out over his territory. He turned as soon as they stepped through the door. "I was expecting to see the two of you. Have a seat."

"I'm not sure I can." Bennett's body was full of tension and nervous energy. He wanted to move. He wanted to act.

"Fair enough." Rex headed to the small bar in the corner and poured a bit of amber liquid into a small glass for each of them. "I think we could use one of these. Shit, you certainly look like you could, Bennett."

"Fuck yes," he growled as he took the glass. "With good reason."

"I won't argue with you." Rex sat down with a sigh, taking the armchair Bennett had refused. "It's not the first time we've had it happen, of course, but things get a little stressful when a human is changed into one of us. We can handle it, but it's always a cause for concern. Annie's situation was no less so, considering the extent of her injuries. Dawn just checked in with me a short while ago, though. She said Annie has fully recovered and is doing well learning about this new side of herself. And Stephanie's okay, too," he added.

A bit of the agitation within him unwound. Bennett wouldn't stop worrying about Stephanie and Annie, but at least he knew nothing disastrous had happened. "That's good, but we've still got a problem to solve. I know you're concerned about the truce between the Silvergroves and us, Rex. I really do get it, but I'd say they've broken their end of the deal. This isn't just about an old feud with them anymore."

"Especially not after that attack at the clinic," Kane added. "That was in broad daylight and against humans. I don't doubt they would've done it even if the clinic had been full of patients. In that sense, we're fortunate that Bennett and Stephanie had taken the preventative measures they did, or we might be looking at a much bigger situation. It would be harder to contain, too."

"Mm. Yes." Rex's face was rigid and distant as he sipped his whiskey.

"I won't take no for an answer this time, Rex." Bennett was pushing it, he knew. This wasn't how someone spoke to a respected Alpha. Rex's reputation was what made this all the more frustrating. "The Bloodmoon Crew will come after Annie and Stephanie to finish the job. Emil Silvergrove is the one who hired me. He told me that Nelson and his men are confident they can have the entire Eugene area under their rule. Humans and shifters alike. This isn't just a one-off incident."

Kane nodded. "Crime has increased lately. I think if we took a closer look at everything through this scope, we'd find that the Crew is responsible for it."

Rex tossed back the last of his shot. He rubbed his lips together as he considered his empty glass. "You're right."

Bennett stared at him for a moment, not sure if

he'd heard him correctly. He'd expected to argue until he was blue in the face. Considering how quickly Rex had shot him down before, that only made sense.

"You're right," Rex repeated, "but the problem is how to pursue this. What they've done is unforgivable and certainly goes beyond the bounds of any truce or treaty we have with them. The problem is that the Bloodmoon Crew is an integral part of the Silvergrove pack. They're the leaders, and they probably have at least some percentage of their membership following them loyally regardless of what someone else told you."

"But it's definitely not all of them," Bennett insisted. "If it was just Emil, he could leave and join another pack. He told me about entire families suffering under Nelson's rule, forced to pay for protection or work in his criminal schemes. They have to do it or face the consequences."

"Yes, but how do we determine who those people are?" Rex asked calmly. "I'm willing to get out there and do this, Bennett. I want to be clear on that, but I also want to make sure we're being smart about it and forming some sort of strategy. Battling half a pack isn't the same as battling an entire one."

"We had a similar experience with the Morwoods," Kane reminded him.

"Yes, but we didn't know what we were getting into with that. We didn't know they were only supporting their leader because he'd put them under a spell. From our point of view, they were all still one entity. If we go in and take out anyone who stands in our way, we very well might be fighting those who are forced to do so. I don't think that would make us any better than Nelson Silvergrove himself."

Bennett balled his hands into fists. He completely understood what Rex was saying, but it made him feel more defeated than ever. "I'm not sure how we can possibly understand who's on our side in a battle situation."

"I might be able to help."

He turned, but he already knew it would be Stephanie standing in the doorway as soon as he'd heard her words. Her voice was a bit shaky, and dark half-moons sat under her eyes, even though she'd slept for a bit. She looked completely exhausted, and all Bennett wanted to do was pull her close and show her just how much he yearned to take care of her.

Rex stood and waved to the chair he'd just

vacated. "Please, have a seat. Can I get you anything to drink? I pride myself on keeping some top-shelf whiskey in the cabinet."

Stephanie looked up at Bennett as she passed him. "No, thanks. I'm good."

"The offer stands if you change your mind. I know things have been stressful for you." Rex leaned against the fireplace. "In light of that, I hate for you to be involved in this at all, but I'm curious. How can you help?"

Bennett watched her as she sat in that chair. Stephanie was a practical person, the sort who cared about function more than form, yet still looked so beautiful and graceful. He knew it'd been the right thing to bring her and Annie to the packhouse. It was the safest place for them—perhaps even safer than his own cabin at the moment—and Annie needed everything that could be offered there. Yet Bennett wanted nothing more than to be alone with her.

Stephanie took a deep breath. "I know this sounds odd, although maybe it's not that crazy considering everything I've witnessed today. Anyway, I'm an animal psychic."

The room was thick and heavy for a moment. Bennett took a step toward her and then stopped, not wanting to crowd or be too pushy. Kane had given him good advice earlier. As much as he wanted to set their relationship in concrete, this wasn't the time. "What do you mean?"

"For a long time, I've known there's more to my success rate at the clinic than my alternative modalities. I can actually communicate with the animals and get their input on how they feel." Stephanie looked desperate as she glanced around the room. "I know it sounds insane."

"No, it doesn't," Bennett said softly.

"Not at all," Rex agreed. "The wolves in a pack are able to communicate telepathically with each other. I think, out of anyone you could tell this to, we're probably the most receptive."

"Yes, I've just learned quite a bit about that." Stephanie picked gently at the upholstery. "Annie was able to shift. I won't waste your time by describing it since you already know, but one of the most remarkable things was that I could still talk to her while she was in her wolf form."

"Really?" Bennett's heart had been twisted in all sorts of directions, and now it bent toward hope. Nothing could be more important to Stephanie than her daughter, and his carelessness had changed

Annie forever. This, however, was a new angle he'd never imagined.

Stephanie pressed her lips together as she nodded. "Really. With dogs, it's just pictures and emotions. It's not like they understand English beyond a few words. Bennett, when Rambo looks at you, I can get all sorts of warm, happy feelings. But when I spoke to Annie—" she broke off and looked at the floor.

"I hadn't thought about that before," Rex murmured. "A psychic getting through our telepathic link."

"Could this be because there's already a link, with them being mother and daughter?" Kane questioned. "I'm not trying to be dismissive of any of this, but I want to understand how far it could go."

"Yes," Rex agreed. "That's very important."

"That became the topic once I told Joan and the others what was happening," Stephanie explained. "We decided to do a little experiment, and I could speak fluently with anyone in the room as long as they were in wolf form. With what little I understand about who attacked us, I thought you should know."

Rex scratched his jaw. "You'd be able to read the minds of the Silvergroves and figure out who genuinely has bad intentions toward us and who doesn't."

"That's the idea," she agreed.

Bennett could hear the fear in her voice, and his wolf hated it. "You can't do that, Stephanie. Shifter battles aren't just a few punches thrown in a dark parking lot. People die."

"I know." Stephanie's nails now worked at the hem of her shirt. "Annie almost did already. I don't want to see that happen again."

"We can find some better way to do this," Bennett insisted.

Rex straightened. "Stephanie, you could be very crucial to the plan. We'll have to hammer out some details regardless, but I'll need to know for sure that you're willing to commit to this. You'll probably see people die, and it won't be pretty. You're also taking the risk yourself, too."

She nodded. "I understand."

Bennett met her gaze. He wanted to tell her this was crazy. She could've already been killed earlier that day at her clinic, and what she was about to head into was far more dangerous. He'd failed to protect her once and couldn't let that happen again.

But he saw everything in those green eyes: sadness and loss mixed with hope and determination. Bennett was willing to go to battle, to lay his life on the line, but Stephanie could fight for Annie and herself in a way he couldn't. As much as it pained him, he knew it was up to her. He gave her the slightest nod.

"All right," Rex said with a clap of his hands. "Then it's time to get down to brass tacks and figure out exactly what we're going to do."

Stephanie fidgeted in her seat. "I think I'll take that whiskey after all."

15

"Mom." Annie took Stephanie's hand and held it tightly. "It doesn't feel right to let you go out there and do this."

"I think Bennett feels the same way, though he hasn't said it." Stephanie smiled. She'd noticed how much he'd held himself back when she'd come to Rex's den to explain what she could do. "He doesn't think it's a good idea for a human to be part of a battle among wolves. He's probably right, but sometimes we have to do the hard things."

Annie sat on the edge of the bed in the room the Glenwoods had given her right next to Stephanie's. She'd showered and eaten and even had a little rest, though she looked very pale. The dogs had stayed by her side as much as possible, and they snoozed on the floor. "I know. You've always said that, although I never thought the hard things would be quite like this."

Stephanie sucked in a breath. "Me, neither."

"I think what feels extra hard right now is that I can't go with you." Annie put her clasped hands on her knee. "It makes sense, and I get that. I'd really just be in the way right now, but I feel terrible that you have to go do this alone."

"I'm not alone." Stephanie was terrified, truth be told. No matter how much they explained everything to her, she didn't really know what she was getting into. The one thing she could be sure of was that the Glenwoods wouldn't just leave her to her own devices. "Bennett will be there with me, along with everyone else."

"Yeah, he looks like he's about to explode," Annie commented.

"What do you mean?"

Annie gave her a look. "How many times do we have to have this conversation, Mom? He's keeping his distance right now, but he's nuts for you, and this whole thing is driving him crazy. I saw him for about five seconds, and I can tell. And it's not just because you're a human."

"Now, who's the psychic?" Stephanie teased.

"Let's just get surviving out of the way, then we can figure out the rest. You'll be okay staying here?"

"I think so. I was a little put out at first, feeling like the weakling being left behind. But apparently, this is where all the little ones are brought in times of danger, so I get to help out. I'm kind of excited about that." Annie was beaming.

"Perfect." Stephanie kissed her forehead and stood up. "I'll be back as soon as possible. Don't push yourself too hard."

When she stepped out into the hallway, she nearly ran into Bennett. He'd lifted his hand to knock but put his arm around Stephanie as she collided with him. "I was just coming to see if you were ready to go. I'll drive you out there since the others will be going on foot. Timing is important."

"Yes, I'm ready." Her stomach was in her throat as they got into his SUV. "Thank you."

He let out a gruff noise as they sped out onto the highway. "I hardly see any reason for you to thank me, given the circumstances."

"You made sure Annie was safe," she pointed out firmly. "She might not be alive right now if it hadn't been for you and Kane getting there when you did, and of course, I never would've known what the bite would do to her."

Bennett was silent for a time. "I'm glad she's okay."

He didn't want to take any credit for it, and Stephanie decided not to push him. Bennett had put up some sort of wall between them sometime at the packhouse, though she hadn't been sure why. She definitely felt the distance there, as though he'd pulled back from her as soon as he knew Annie was going to live.

He turned off the highway and onto a side road. "Remember everything Rex told you," he said, his eyes fiercely on the road ahead. "On two legs, you'll be like a beacon to the Bloodmoon Crew. The rest of us all know that and will be doing everything we can to defend you, but make sure you don't get yourself into a bad position. And actually...." He trailed off as he rubbed his hand over his mouth.

"What?"

"I'd like you to stay near me," he finished. "You were the one who volunteered to do this, but I still feel a certain amount of responsibility for you."

It was hard to think of anything as being sweet when they were heading straight into the jaws of danger, but she still did. "Sure."

"Here we are." He turned up a driveway not so different from the Glenwoods'.

This one was closer to town and had a more modern feel, with hard edges and oddly placed windows. Several cars were parked in the driveway, and Stephanie noticed they were all high-end.

Bennett screeched to a stop as he spotted the rest of his pack members come streaking out of the woods. "It's time."

"I'm with you." Her mouth tasted like copper as she commanded her body to do what they'd discussed. Stephanie jumped out of the truck. She ran at Bennett's side, sticking close and paying attention to everything around her. She opened her mind, willing herself to allow in any psychic energies that could be found. They'd only had a little time to experiment with this new revelation before it was time to head out, not wanting to give the Bloodmoon Crew any further chances at retaliation. It'd worked well in the comfort and safety of the packhouse, but what would it be like out there?

Bennett transformed as he ran beside her. It looked like he was stumbling for a moment, but the awkwardness of the shift lasted for only a fraction of a second before his hands touched the ground as paws. It was quick, far faster than what Annie had been able to do, and he was soon another one of the

Glenwood wolves speeding toward the Silvergrove packhouse.

They must have been expecting them. The doors opened. Wolves burst out with their teeth bared. Others, still in their human forms, were right on their heels, making their transition as they ran forward to clash with the Glenwoods.

Stay focused. Bennett's voice was gritty in her head. *Just see what you can pick up, and make sure you let me know.*

I'll try. I don't know if I can talk to this many people at once. She'd hardly had any time to get used to this idea, much less understand how it all worked. What had been dismissed back at the packhouse as things they would work out on the battlefield now seemed like much more than minor details.

You can only do what you can do, and no one expects more of you than that. It's the same for all of us. We just have to use our talents the best we can. Bennett joined the Glenwoods at the back of the pack as they moved up into the expansive lawn.

Right. They both had their secrets, and now it was time to put those secrets to use.

She opened her mind. It didn't feel the same as reading a dachshund's feelings or reaching out to her daughter. It wasn't even the same as touching the minds of the Glenwood women in the safety of the packhouse. It was complete chaos.

There! Over there!

Kill them all!

Don't let them get around the back of the house!

Stephanie relayed this last one to Bennett. It was the one that stood out amongst the noise inside her head, the one that seemed relevant.

Good. Keep going, he encouraged.

The mayhem inside her mind was nearly making her dizzy. Everyone was speaking at once. She heard the Silvergroves as well as the Glenwoods, and it was too much. Then there was the sheer horror of what was actually happening. Wolves pounced on one another, ripping with their teeth and claws. Blood soaked into the ground and matted into fur. Her instinct was to stop this whole thing and patch them up, to get them on her exam table and fix them. She'd spent her entire adult life training to keep these kinds of horrible wounds from killing animals, and there wasn't a damn thing she could do about it. Stephanie had been warned that people would die, and it was already happening. She wasn't going to be able to do this.

Yes, you can.

Stephanie hadn't realized she'd let that part

outside of her mind. She put a hand on Bennett's shoulder and steadied herself. He was right. She'd done plenty of other things in her life, and some of them were damn hard. She was doing this for Annie's future as well as that of anyone else under the crushing control of the Bloodmoon Crew. She had to make it work. The scene in front of her would only keep happening unless she did.

She lasered in her focus, drowning everyone out as she concentrated on one wolf up near the Silvergrove garage. Wolves were fighting all around him. Blood was flying and teeth were flashing. He was bobbing his head up and down as he tried to figure out where to enter the fray. *I don't want to do this. But he'll kill me if I don't. I literally have to kill or be killed. This is horrible.*

That one. He doesn't want to fight. Stephanie fixated on the hesitant Silvergrove, hoping she could successfully explain who she meant amongst a sea of gray fur. *He's only doing it because they'll kill him otherwise.*

Tell him to come around behind us.

Stephanie jumped as she realized that was Rex inside her mind. Was she broadcasting to all the Glenwoods?

Don't worry about it, came a youthful voice that was far too chipper for the situation. *I've got him.*

The wolf in question popped out of existence completely and reappeared behind the Glenwood lines. *What the fuck was that?*

Stephanie wondered the same thing, but she reached out to him with the one thing she did know. *You're safe now.*

That was Ava, Bennett explained. *As I said, we each have our own talents.*

Stephanie glanced to her left to see Joan, Dawn, and Ava, the teen girl who'd kept the dogs wrangled, standing with their shoulders together. Bright balls of fiery light shot from their hands, whizzing over the battlefield and exploding into the sides of the packhouse.

Keep going, Bennett reminded her.

The thrill of one life saved sent a bolt of adrenaline through her. She spotted a wolf defending the front of the pack house. The chill rippling down her spine had nothing to do with the cold evening air. She never would've guessed she could recognize one wolf out of dozens, but she knew who this was.

Just remember, boys, the more we kill here today, the fewer we have to hunt down like cowering mutts tomorrow. Images from his mind flashed through

Stephanie's, ones of all the terrified people he'd been threatening or worse. One of them was far too familiar.

Her fingers scrunched in Bennett's fur. *That's the one who bit Annie.*

As soon as she let that thought fly, she knew exactly what would happen. A new surge of Glenwood energy moved through the battle, and the dark wolf disappeared. Stephanie turned her head. She knew the bastard deserved everything he got, but it was hard to watch. Her stomach rolled.

You're doing great.

That was Bennett again. Stephanie sucked in a deep breath. He was making all the difference in her powers, strengthening them as she stood beside him. The mental switchboard she was operating couldn't have happened if he wasn't there, and she knew it. But that didn't make the results of it all any easier to stomach.

Bennett angled his long body in front of Stephanie, scooting her back as two wolves came tumbling through the masses, teeth bared and claws shredding.

Stephanie took a deep breath. They'd saved one, at least. Maybe she could find more. That was what she had to hang her hope on now.

Please! I don't want to fight you! If only you could hear me. This came from a wolf scrambling with a pure white Glenwood, one that Stephanie now knew to be Lori. She relayed those thoughts to the pack Luna, and she instantly backed off.

One by one, Stephanie continued to find them. It scared the hell out of them when she replied, but then Stephanie got to feel that ultimate relief that flooded through their bodies as soon as they knew they were safe.

There are so many of them! Why is he making us do this?

That bastard. I ought to turn around and kill him myself, but I'd never be able to alone.

I don't know who my allies are here.

Why does anyone follow him voluntarily?

My baby. He's going to kill my baby if I don't do this.

Her heart wrenched as she identified them, spreading the word to the Glenwoods. Some were quickly transported through Ava's magic. Others were defended with magic from the other women until they could get to safety. The Glenwoods refused to fight those who were forced into this and moved on, leaving the innocent Silvergroves bewildered but thankful. Just as Joan and the others were flinging their magic, Stephanie was flinging thoughts, feelings, and images throughout the battle. She tuned out the sounds and the smells of the wolves who continued to fight, keeping her mind only on the mental aspect as much as possible.

There she is!

Stephanie picked up on the impression when it was too late. A wolf dove through the melee. His yellow eyes were zeroed in on her. The white of his teeth chilled her to the bone as his strong legs lifted his massive paws off the ground. This was it. She'd saved lives, but she was going to die.

Bennett slammed the wolf into the ground. It fought back hard, striking out with sharp claws. Bennett pinned it by the neck, and saliva dripped from his teeth as he and his foe exchanged blows. Blood gushed from a newly opened cut on Bennett's neck, pouring down into the other wolf's face. Bennett backed off, allowing the other wolf to rise.

Stephanie screamed. He had saved her, but now he would pay the ultimate price.

Just wait. A Glenwood came alongside her, steadying her and stepping into Bennett's place. It was Kane.

It happened so quickly, but the world was in slow motion around her. Bennett's opponent was on his feet and charging. Its feet left the ground as it leaped toward him, just as it had lunged toward Stephanie a moment ago. With the power of his hind legs, Bennett shot forward, his teeth clamping around the other wolf's neck. He forcefully flicked his head down and to the side, flinging the limp body of his enemy to the ground for the last time.

Bennett quickly rejoined her. *Nothing to worry about.*

I'm not so sure about that. It'd been petrifying to see that, and for a moment, she hadn't thought Bennett would live. He'd proven otherwise, but this wasn't over. The Silvergrove numbers had dwindled, but they still rallied.

A dark wolf, nearly black, stood at the center of them as they continued to push back. *Don't back down!* he insisted. *The Glenwoods were fools for thinking there could ever truly be peace between us. Truces and alliances are for cowards, as they've already proven themselves to be.*

Anger simmered inside her. Stephanie knew they weren't cowards at all. It took no effort for her to relay everything to Bennett and the others.

We're the Bloodmoon Crew! Nelson cried out in his mind. *These bastards have helped us separate the wheat from the chaff. Now it's time to show them what we're*

really made of. Don't stop fighting until every last Glen-
wood is dead!

A new sense of energy swelled through the pack. No honorable wolves were left to sort out. Some now even fought alongside those considered enemies only a short time ago. Cries of pain ripped through the air, and the scent of blood was thick.

As the sun set behind the Silvergrove packhouse, the Bloodmoon Crew fell.

16

"It's over. You can relax a little." Bennett smiled at his mate.

Stephanie didn't quite understand how he could be smiling after that. Then, she had to remember who he was and what he did for a living. "I'll try, but I'm not making any promises. What are they doing over there?" She gestured with her chin at Rex, Brody, and Max standing near the front of the Silvergrove packhouse, appearing to be deep in discussion with a few people she didn't recognize.

"They're working things out with the remaining Silvergroves, the ones you helped save." He pointed at one man with auburn hair. "That's Emil, the guy who had asked for my help in the first place."

"You took out the Bloodmoon Crew," Stephanie

replied, "so what does that leave for them to work out?" She was exhausted, both mentally and physically. Her mind had been bent and twisted one way and another as she worked her psychic powers harder than she ever had before. Understanding and absorbing everything around her was enough of a challenge, even without that.

Though he looked a bit worse for wear, Bennett wasn't as weary as she was. The cut she'd seen on his neck before had already healed and was now nothing more than a pink line on his skin. "We can't just leave them to fend for themselves, not when their pack has been completely turned upside down. Without at least some guidance, the remainder of their pack could easily end up having the same troubles all over again. Rex will help them reorganize, figure out who the next Alpha should be, and provide whatever assistance they may need."

"Wow. It seems your pack is more generous to its enemies than most people are to their friends." Not that it should really surprise her all that much, given everything she'd already noticed about the Glenwoods concerning herself and Annie. They were impressive in so many ways.

"Yeah, I'd say that sums it up pretty well. They've got this, so I should get you back to the packhouse."

Bennett began guiding the way back toward the truck.

"Stephanie."

She looked up. The woman who had called to her was a familiar face from long ago. More lines creased around her mouth and eyes, and Stephanie remembered her as having the same dark hair as Bennett. It was now mostly gray. If Stephanie had run into her in the supermarket, she might not recognize her at all. There, she knew instantly.

"Stephanie, you remember my mother, Patricia," Bennett said.

"Of course." She swallowed, recalling instantly what he'd told her about why he'd broken up with her. A new jolt of discomfort moved through her as she stood facing Patricia. Stephanie hadn't known back then, but she knew now.

"I'd like to talk to you for a moment if I could." Mrs. Westbrook glanced up at her son. "Alone."

To Stephanie's surprise, Bennett smiled. He gave Stephanie a reassuring squeeze on the arm. "Sure. I'll go see if they need my help with anything."

Stephanie glared at him as he retreated. She was a grown woman, and her veterinary practice had trained her not to take anyone's nasty words or insulting treatment personally, but this was different.

Patricia wasn't just an unsatisfied customer or someone who thought their Havanese was more special than anyone else's.

"You look tired, dear. Let's have a seat." Patricia led the way to a small seating area off the side of the Silvergrove packhouse, lit by the yellow glow of porch lamps.

It felt wrong to just sit down on the porch while everyone around them was working to clean up the aftermath of the battle, but her body easily sank onto the chair. Stephanie braced herself, unsure of what to expect from Patricia.

"You were incredible today," she began, pressing her hands between her knees and watching as Rex, Bennett, and the others conferred with the other pack. "I'm very familiar with the telepathic link among packmates, but this was something on a completely different level. It was very impressive, and you really made a difference here."

"Thank you, but it's not like I was the one doing the heavy lifting. That was everyone else." She looked out at the yard and then away again, knowing what had made the dark stains in the dry grass.

"You changed lives today, Stephanie. Don't deny yourself that."

"There wasn't much of a choice. I couldn't ever

be guaranteed that they wouldn't come after my daughter again. I'd do anything for Annie, and apparently, that includes helping a pack of wolves win a battle against another." She let out an ironic snort of laughter that held no real humor in it.

"Yes. I heard about that. I can't imagine what it must feel like for you to know what your child has had to go through." Patricia sat back and looked up at the moon. "Actually, in a way, I can."

Stephanie waited, watching her expectantly.

"It's not the exact same thing, of course, but as a parent, I can see the parallels. It's hard to see your child suffer. It's even harder when you know it's your fault. That last part is what I've been dealing with for a long time. I owe you an apology."

"It was a long time ago," Stephanie replied. "We were different people back then."

"But it doesn't change what you and Bennett had together. Don't get me wrong, either. I'm not telling you this simply because you proved yourself useful to the pack tonight. That's great, but it's incidental compared to what's been in my heart." Patricia looked straight at Stephanie now, her eyes glimmering with tears in the moonlight. "I let my own fears and biases get in the way of love and happiness. I couldn't have predicted the future, and most people aren't lucky enough to find the love of their life when they're just teenagers. I can give myself all the excuses I want, and I have, but that's all they are. Excuses."

Patricia chewed her lip and looked down at her hands. "We tend to create an identity based on who we are and how we grew up. We wolves, usually, are very close-knit. We want the same for our children because we can see the benefit and safety in keeping those you can trust around you. Bennett's father and I wanted to protect him. We wanted him to have the best life he possibly could. That was why we got scared about you. A relationship between a shifter and a human isn't going to be without its problems."

"I think that's true of any kind of relationship," Stephanie replied dryly. Patricia seemed truly sorry, but it still stung a little to know how much she'd been judged.

"You're absolutely right," Patricia admitted. "We tried so hard to give Bennett a good life that we messed it up completely. He was *happy* with you, Stephanie. I haven't seen that sort of happiness in him since then. Not as he worked his way through the academy, and not as he worked his way up in the police force. Sure, there were some good times and some smiles, but it was like the light in his eyes had just gone out. I know without question he hasn't been happy these last few years, doing this mercenary work that scares the hell out of me. I can't help but think it all might've been vastly different if you'd been a part of his life all this time."

"That's a lot of pressure to put on someone," Stephanie said slowly. She watched Bennett as he talked about who knew what to Brody. From there, he looked handsome and confident, not like the picture his mother painted. "To think they might've completely altered decades of a person's life."

Patricia nodded. "Yes, and maybe I'm just being romantic. But the fact is I see that light again. Even in the face of a war with the Silvergroves, the Bloodmoon Crew coming after you, and how much he worried for Annie, he's different inside."

Stephanie would never be able to see it from her perspective since she hadn't known Bennett in the intervening years Patricia spoke of. She believed her, but it was easy to think life was all sunshine and roses after having gone through days as traumatic as the last few had been. "I appreciate you telling me all of this, Patricia. I really do, and I know it comes from the heart. The thing is, I'm still a human. Bennett is still a shifter. Whatever else has changed in our lives, that hasn't."

"True," she said with a solemn nod. "I can see now that there's much more to being one of us than just the ability to turn into a wolf. The dedication and teamwork you've shown today prove that, Stephanie. I sincerely hope you'll accept my apology someday, even if not today."

She hesitated, uncertain of what to say. She'd certainly felt like a part of things out there, communicating with everyone and making sure the Bloodmoon Crew went down without taking too many innocent lives with them. For a few minutes, she hadn't been thinking about who was what species and how that affected the other. It'd been about so much more than that. Patricia knew that now, even if she hadn't in the past. Stephanie smiled at her. "Yes, I suppose you're right. And I do accept your apology. It means a lot to me."

Patricia's shoulders fell with relief. "I should be thanking you for getting that off my mind. Now, I won't turn around and try to tell you what to do with your life, Stephanie. You've got a lot going on, especially with Annie. I just want you to know you have my full support and acceptance, no matter what."

"Thank you." Up until recently, Stephanie hadn't often thought about the young girl inside her who was so bitter and hurt when her boyfriend had dumped her without reason. Now, though, she could feel just how much that girl was healing.

Bennett stepped up onto the porch. "There's not much more here for me to do. Stephanie, I should get you back to Annie."

"Yes. I'd like that. It was nice talking to you, Patricia." Stephanie gave her a friendly nod as she followed Bennett back to his vehicle.

Back at the Glenwood packhouse, Stephanie rushed to find Annie. She found her in the living room with several small children gathered around her. Crayons and blocks were strewn everywhere, and Annie looked thrilled. So did the dogs. Sherlock was lying on his side on the floor, serving as a pillow to a little boy reading a book. A couple of girls were trying doll clothes on Jacques, and Penelope was looking after them all as though they were her own pups.

Annie hopped up off the floor. "Mom, you're back! I already heard about what you did."

"We don't need to talk about me," Stephanie deflected. Her brain was too tired to think about the battle and her psychic powers. "Tell me about *you*. Are you still feeling okay?"

"I'm great, Mom. In fact, I don't think I've ever felt better in my life, and these kids are so sweet! Oh, and guess what?" Annie grabbed Stephanie's hands, her eyes wide and happy.

"What?" Stephanie asked, laughing at seeing how excited she was.

"They said they'll make me a part of the pack if I want to be. Isn't that amazing? Like, I know my life is still going to be so weird, but I'll have everyone here to help me. It's so cool!" Annie was practically jumping up and down.

Considering she'd been bleeding out not all that long ago, there was no question she was healed. Stephanie tucked a strand of Annie's hair behind her ear. She'd been so worried Annie would be traumatized by this whole thing, but she was acting like she'd won the lottery. "I'm so glad you're happy."

As Annie resumed playing with the children, Stephanie turned to Bennett. "I don't mean to be a burden, but I'd like to ask Rex or Lori if I can stay the night. Annie's fine, but I don't want to leave her just yet."

"You can." Bennett's finger brushed her wrist, stopping short of taking her hand. "Trust me, you don't even need to ask."

17

BENNETT LIFTED HIS FIST TO KNOCK BUT HELD IT there. He took several breaths and then dropped his arm. After chewing his lip for a minute, he lifted his arm again and knocked.

The bedroom door swung open a few seconds later. The smile that spread across Stephanie's face told him he hadn't needed to hesitate that much. "Hi. I was just gathering the few things I've got, getting ready to go home. I figure it's safe now, although I think Annie might be staying here at the packhouse for a while. She's a bit enamored with everyone." She left the door open as she stepped over to the bed.

"It's safe," he agreed. "I was wondering, would you want to take a walk in the woods with me before you go? It's beautiful land almost any time of the year, and you've really only gotten to see the inside of the house."

Stephanie zipped up the small bag Lori had given her for her things. She looked up into his eyes, searching them more deeply than he'd seen her do in a long time. "Sure. That'd be nice."

A few minutes later, they headed out the back door and down the deck stairs. "I know how much you like taking a walk when you need to clear your head, and you've probably had a lot of things to clear out recently."

"That's not an exaggeration." She pressed a hand to her forehead and blinked even as she looked around at the backyard's open space and the trees surrounding it. "I know Annie is doing fine. Better than fine, really, but it's still been a lot to process. Then—wait a second. How did you know I walk to clear my head?"

Bennett tucked his hands in his pockets and grinned. "I may have told you my biggest secret, but it wasn't the only one I was hanging onto. I do happen to know, though, that you'd often go out walking around the farms that weren't too far from your college whenever you'd been cramming for exams or dealing with tough classes."

"But we'd already—" She broke off, and realization dawned on her face. "You were the wolf I always used to see!"

"Guilty as charged," he said with a shrug. "I almost told you before but didn't find the right time."

"Huh." Stephanie's hands swung at her sides as they stepped onto the trail, and she aimed a sideways glance up at him. "So you were spying on me."

"I think 'visiting' is a better term," he replied. "We hadn't been together for a while, and I couldn't just call you and see how you were doing. Not after the way we'd left things."

She looked down to step over a tree root, smiling. "I always thought I had some sort of special connection to that wolf, but at the time, I thought I was just being a silly girl who'd spent too much time in a lab."

"There was probably some of that," he said. "I was probably even counting on you thinking of it that way. You always were good with animals."

"And you're such a beast!" She laughed and poked his arm. "It's nice to know you were thinking about me, though. I thought about you every now and then, too."

He hadn't had the chance to spend time with her

like this, when they didn't have to worry about their safety or what might happen next. It'd been amazing just to see her again, but it felt altogether different under their current circumstances. That didn't mean he could just relax, though, not when so much still hung in the balance.

Bennett caught her hand and slid his fingers down between hers. "Leaving you was the hardest thing I ever had to do, Stephanie. I know you understand the circumstances, and there's not much we can do about it now, but I just want you to know that it really did change my life. At the time, I thought I was meant to be with you, and I should've fought harder for that."

Stephanie stopped and turned to him, looking up into his eyes.

After a minute, he couldn't help but laugh. "What? Haven't you had enough time to see just how much I've aged?"

"It's not that. And actually, I think you're even more handsome than you were as a kid." She reached up and touched his face, her fingers tender. "I was just looking for something."

His heart thundered and his wolf churned. No longer was he stuck in protective mode, constantly on the watch to make sure no threats could get to her. He could only focus on how it felt to be with her, to feel that connection that had never gone away. In fact, he was sure it had deepened. "Did you find it?"

She was trying to keep her face in check, and her mouth squirmed as she fought her smile from getting wider, but she was losing. "Yeah. I did."

Bennett clasped her other hand and pulled her close. "Stephanie, I know you have to go back to your regular life now, or at least as regular as it can be after all this. I'm not even sure what normal will mean for me now. The only thing I do know is that I don't want to lose you again."

She tipped her head curiously. "Not that I'm not happy to hear you say that, but I'm a bit surprised. After we'd brought Annie to the packhouse, you seemed a bit distant. I'd been thinking there was something between us, but then you pulled back."

"That's not what I meant to do, not really." Bennett turned and continued along the trail, still holding her hand. It was easier to talk when they were moving. "I wanted to support you and help Annie, and I didn't want to pressure you with talk about our future or exactly what we were to each other. You didn't need a lover right then. You needed a partner."

"Wow." Stephanie's fingers squeezed his for a moment. "They make movies about guys who say things like that, but they're always fictional. They're not usually wolves or vigilantes, though."

"See, that's why they're fictional. They only have some of the details right." This was so much like what he remembered from their younger days. He and Stephanie didn't have to be doing anything significant to have a good time. They just had to be together, and they could banter all day. It was nice to see that even though many things had changed, that hadn't.

"Well, it was sweet of you. And you were right. My mind was completely on Annie, and I wouldn't have been much good if you wanted to talk about something as simple as my favorite color."

"Yellow," he replied automatically. "Or at least it used to be."

"I can't believe you remember that." Her body brushed closely against his as the trail narrowed for a moment, and they climbed slowly through the hills of the Glenwood territory.

"I remember a lot." They reached a small clearing, one where the pine trees grew close and had dropped their needles into a thick bed on the forest floor. A singular tree grew near the center, and he moved toward it. "I never forgot you, Stephanie. I honestly believe we're fated to be together, and I want to ask you to be my true mate. But I want to make sure you know what that means."

She paused as they neared the center tree, her free hand drifting over the rough bark. "It sounds like I still have plenty to learn, but I always was a good student."

Selene, help him. It would be so easy to just press her up against that tree and show her how he felt about her, but he'd brought her out there to discuss this. Bennett didn't want to miss his chance. "We're connected. We've already talked about that, how fate has strung us together. I won't ever truly be complete until I have you by my side, but our traditions call for more than just a faithful rela-tionship."

Stephanie leaned against the tree. "Tell me."

How had he spent all these years without the privilege of looking at that beautiful face? Of feeling her luscious body against his? "In our pack, we mark our mates. That means that I would bite you, just here." Bennett pushed aside her flannel and touched the slope of her shoulder, where it peeked out around her tank top. It was *his* flannel, actually, and his undershirt that she'd gotten washed at the packhouse, and he experienced the thrill of her being in his clothes all over again.

She looked down at where his finger touched her. "Bite me?"

"Yes, with my fangs. It has to be deep for it to take. The thing is, once I do that, you'll become one of us. A shifter." He trailed his fingers down her arm and took her hand again, watching her face carefully. "Then we'd consummate our relationship, and the bond would be complete."

"Oh." Emotions moved across her face, twisting her mouth and tweaking her eyebrows as she considered everything he'd just revealed to her. "I'd become a wolf?"

"Yes." He'd paced the room he'd stayed in at the packhouse, trying to decide the best way to describe all of this to her without freaking her out. Stephanie wasn't a delicate, sensitive woman. She'd gone through veterinary school and dealt with life and death every day. But she'd seen so much in the past week that was completely beyond the scope of her reality. "It would take some adjustment, just as it will for Annie, but it doesn't mean you can't still have your practice and live your life the way you want to. Far more shifters are around here than anyone realizes."

"Yes, and they're nurses, policemen, and firefighters," she said with a nervous laugh. "Bennett, I think I've been making some assumptions about your life without meaning to. When I found out about you, I thought it was only something you could be born with. Then, when Annie was bitten, I concluded these things could also happen accidentally. Now you're telling me that some people, ones who've been chosen by destiny, have the chance at doing this voluntarily?"

Leave it to her to analyze it in such a way, but she was right. "Yes. Most packs nowadays don't practice marking, but the Glenwoods have held onto the tradition. It's a way of being truly bonded with your mate and deepening your feelings for each other."

She touched his face again, her thumb moving softly over the corner of his mouth. "It's hard to imagine feeling any more deeply for you than I already do."

"I know." Bennett closed his eyes and rested his forehead against hers. It felt so incredible just to be standing there with her, to know their feelings for each other were strong enough to make it through all the obstacles life and the Bloodmoon Crew had put before them. A deep sense of satisfaction radiated through him, and he hadn't been able to stop thinking about how much better it could be.

He lifted his head and took her face into his hands, looking deeply into her eyes. "Stephanie, I know this is a lot to think about, but I'd like you to consider it at least. I'm not asking you for an answer, not now and maybe not for a long time. I want you to be sure."

She leaned into his hand. "I've only ever known how to be human. That was all I knew existed, after all. But I can see just how much there is to life as a shifter. You've got such a close connection with your pack, and you have all the love and support that goes along with it. I was an outsider experiencing that, and I was still so impressed. Then you've got that other side of yourself, the one that knows there's much more to modern life than just staying inside the same four walls or even the same body form."

He smiled. She was still very much a human, yet she understood. Maybe it was because of the psychic connection she'd been able to build with the pack during the battle, but she grasped the idea fairly well. There was so much more, of course, but some of it was impossible to describe. It had to be felt and experienced. "Exactly. It's an exciting life, but I know it's a lot to ask. Like I said, I just want you to think about it and let me know what you decide." He turned away from the tree, his fingers still entwined with hers.

Stephanie's hand pulled back on his, and when he turned, she was still leaning against the tree. "I've thought about it."

An answer that quick had to be bad, but the sunny look on her face gave him hope. "You should give yourself more time."

"No." She pulled him back toward her. "I've already been thinking about it, maybe since before I even knew about the whole idea. My life as a human has been setting me up for this. I'm fascinated by animals, not only in how to help them medically but in how they communicate. When that mysterious wolf was visiting me back in college, I'd started to realize I had more of a connection with the animal world than any of the other students. I would've been laughed right off campus if I'd told anyone I'd had private conversations with a wolf, but I knew I had. It was you, Bennett. Being with you unlocked this thing inside me. I felt that again when we battled the Silvergroves. As long as I had you beside me, I could do all of it. There has to be a reason for that, not the least of which is how much I love you."

He captured her mouth in his, exploring her

velvety lips as he pressed his body against hers. Could she ever possibly know how much all of that meant to him? That he was just as important in her life as she was in his? Bennett pulled back just enough to speak again. "I love you, too. You're sure?"

"Bennett, it would be an honor to become part of your pack and have my true love by my side the whole time I learned about my new inner wolf. Yes. Now that I know we can, I don't want to wait any longer."

His heartbeat pounded in his ears as she readjusted her flannel. There was too much adrenaline running through his system for the sharp pain in his mouth to bother him. Bennett moved forward to hold her between himself and the tree as his vision focused on that delicate curve of flesh.

The bite would come, but first, he traced his lips over that special spot on her shoulder, one that would never be the same again. She wanted him, and she wanted him now. Not just him as a man, but him as a wolf and all that came with it. Bennett had seen the certainty in her eyes and knew she meant everything she said. There could be no bigger turn-on than knowing he would finally, truly, be with his mate.

His gums burned as his fangs descended. He

didn't want to hurt her, but they'd been through so much more pain than this to be together. He opened his mouth and sank his teeth into her flesh.

She held him tightly, a gasp of pain hissing through her teeth as Bennett pressed down harder, ensuring that it was deep enough. Stephanie's hands tightened around him as the pain moved through her, and then they went slack.

The tree was serving as a support, but Bennett quickly grabbed her arms and looked into her eyes. "Are you all right?"

To his surprise, she was smiling. "Yeah, actually."

"I hope it didn't hurt too badly." He kissed the fresh wound, knowing it would heal quickly but still feeling a twinge of guilt.

"It did, but I know it's worth it," she replied, echoing his thoughts from a moment ago. "And this means soon enough, I'll be able to bite you back."

Bennett wiggled his eyebrows. "I look forward to it." He pulled off his jacket and laid it on the soft bed of pine needles that surrounded them. Her flannel appeared in his hand, and he added it to the makeshift pallet. Turning back, he pulled Stephanie into his arms and kissed her deeply. Somehow, this kiss felt different than any of the others. Bennett could feel the connection between them growing stronger already, and he was eager to see just how far they could take it. His arm muscles flexed as he held her tightly against him, knowing he would never have to let her go again. As their tongues twined together, his hands explored the rest of her body. He circled his fingers around her braid and slid down it, feeling each glossy twist of silken hair. His other hand worked down her spine to her lower back, where he scrunched the fabric of her shirt until it loosened from the waistband of her jeans. Her breasts against his chest sent a thrill through his stomach. There were still several layers of clothing between them, but the way she pressed herself against his hardness was enough to drive him wild.

She pulled back and looked up at him with eyes the same tranquil green as the pines around them but full of mischief. Her fingers tugged playfully at the waistband of his jeans. "Just how alone are we out here, anyway?"

"Very," he replied huskily. "Like there's no one in the world but the two of us."

"Good." With eager hands, she freed him from his clothes. Each garment added to the pile on the ground, making their bed for them as they undressed. The fresh air was cool against his skin, but the heat she created inside him blasted any chill away.

When she'd freed him of his shirt and jeans, Stephanie paused. She took half a step back as her eyes swept admiringly over him. He stood before her in only his boxer briefs, and she slid her hands up the sides of them and then across the front. Her palm enticed him as it lingered over his package. "I like these on you," she said as she moved up toward the elastic, "but I like them even better off."

Bennett could hardly control himself once she'd stripped him down. He undressed her quickly, deciding that if they lingered on each other, it would be once they had nothing else standing in their way. Her clothes went into the pile, and Bennett pulled her down onto it with him.

They kissed again, their hands roving and appreciating each other. Her fingers streaked through his hair, and his palms caressed the abundant curves of her backside. Stephanie's attentions roved down and across his shoulders, her fingertips playing with the muscles she found there. Bennett stroked her arms and glided his hands over her breasts.

Stephanie sat up and moved around so that she straddled his knees, and when she took him into her mouth, the earth spun around him. Bennett let out a ragged moan as her tongue drifted up and down the length of his shaft, playing, enticing. Her hands drifted up to his ribs, across his stomach, and then down the fronts of his thighs. Her breasts were warm and soft against his knees, and she tucked her toes underneath his calves to keep them warm.

When she'd fully bewitched him, Stephanie lifted her head. She scooted up so that she straddled him, her heat so close to his pulsing member. She was sitting up straight, and when she reached up to toss her braid behind her back, Bennett knew he'd never seen anything more stunning than his mate above him with the treetops and puffy clouds behind her.

She guided his length into her slowly, sliding down until he was entirely inside that molten core. Stephanie made long, slow strokes with her hips. Their bodies were never apart for long, rejoining as if by magnetic force.

Bennett felt his building ecstasy, but something else as well. Just as he'd always wanted, the bond between them was getting stronger. Her pleasure resounded within him and returned to her, the sensation building as the cycle continued. He reached up and found the elastic that secured her braid, pulling it out and separating the thick sections until her hair lay across her shoulders and down her back as a thick curtain. He wound the strands around his hands and pulled her down to him, sliding his tongue in her mouth so they could be as joined as possible.

Her moan vibrated against the roof of his mouth as her core tightened around him. Bennett's wolf was close to the surface, and he could feel one rising within her as well. It was soft and beautiful, a little unsure but ready to discover this new world. Their bodies thrust together as they reached the apex of their love and let it go.

Catching his breath, Bennett reached to the side and found her flannel. His flannel. Hell, it didn't matter.

Everything he owned belonged to her now, including him.

EPILOGUE

"I just don't understand what the problem is." A worried Megan Sisney looked down at her cat, Harmony. "I've checked with several other vets, and they've given her different medications, but nothing seems to be helping. I guess it's my fault for trying to go to the cheap vets first, no offense. But everyone I've talked to has recommended you. I hope you can figure this out because I feel so bad for her."

"We'll see what we can do." Stephanie did a quick once-over on the cat, checking her vitals as usual. Harmony was a gorgeous calico, or at least she would be if she hadn't licked half the fur off her body. Her hindquarters showed mostly pink skin with darker patches where her coat would have filled in darker. Only a puff of fur was left at the end of her tail. "Many times, something like this is caused by skin allergies."

"Yes, that's what Dr. Sutton suggested right off the bat. He gave her some allergy meds, but they didn't help." Megan stroked Harmony's head to keep her calm.

"Then we can probably rule that out. We can check for a few other medical conditions." Stephanie ran her hands through the cat's fur and looked into her stunning round eyes. Thanks to her practicing over the last few months, she easily opened her mind and centered her psychic energies on Harmony.

At first, it'd been difficult while she was there at work. Bennett had his own job, so he wasn't there by her side to enhance her natural talents. She had to make them happen on her own, and the chaos of so many animal minds had been difficult. Time helped, just as it did with most things.

It wasn't the same speaking telepathically to cats and dogs as it was to shifters in their wolf forms. Stephanie's patients didn't speak English, and that language barrier had been another step to over-come. She had to use images and feelings, just as she had when she'd first started this journey. She concentrated on the cat's bare skin and how it must feel.

An overwhelming sense of panic tightened Stephanie's chest.

"Is there anything at home that could be stressing her out?" Stephanie asked Megan calmly.

"No, not that I can think of. My boyfriend and I live pretty quiet lives. I work from home, so I'm almost always there."

"Stressors aren't always as obvious to us as they are to animals." Stephanie probed Harmony's mind again, looking for what had caused that alarming sensation. The boyfriend Megan had just spoken of suddenly featured in the stream of consciousness she was receiving. Stephanie saw him from Harmony's perspective, tall as a giant, as he entered through the door. "Have you and your boyfriend lived together for very long? Do he and Harmony get along well?"

"Oh, yes," Megan enthused. "That was actually one of the things that helped me know he was the right one. As soon as he met her, he was loving on her and playing with her. In fact, he's paying for this visit since I couldn't afford it after all the other ones."

"I see." That was a good sign, but Stephanie knew there had to be more. She could do some tests, but what Harmony had already communicated convinced her that this was a displacement behavior turned obsessive by stress.

Harmony seemed to understand what Stephanie was doing, and she knew this strange woman was going to help. Stephanie picked up on the softness of a bed, a safe place where Harmony felt comfortable. Then, it was yanked out from under her. Something loud was keeping her from that warm, happy feeling she'd had before.

"It can take cats much longer to adjust to new surroundings than we imagine. Harmony might get along with your boyfriend just fine, but what else happened when he moved in? I'm thinking things like furniture rearrangement, or maybe her bed got moved."

Megan's eyes widened and she slapped her hand over her mouth. "Holy shit. Harmony's bed *was* moved. It always used to be right next to my desk, but we put some of Mitchell's furniture in the office."

"And where is her bed now?"

"Next to the upright freezer in the utility room." Megan's shoulders sagged. "It's old, and its motor makes a horrible noise. Oh, poor Harmony! No wonder you've been stressing out! I'm so sorry, baby!"

That all lined up perfectly with what Harmony had told Stephanie. "Move her bed to a place where she can be calm and comfortable. Maybe back in your office, even if it's not in the same spot. That will take some readjustment on her part again, but we can help keep her calm with some valerian root, catnip, and chamomile. It'd also be good to talk about her nutrition and a diet that will support her as she grows that lovely coat back."

Harmony was the last client of the day, and she and her owner left feeling much better.

"You know, you really ought to consider advertising your psychic services," Annie observed as she closed down the computer system for the day. "The look on that woman's face as she checked out is plenty of proof that it works."

"No way." Stephanie reached down to ruffle Sherlock between the ears. "It was hard enough to get myself established with my other modalities. If I add 'animal psychic' to my resume, it will turn into a circus around here. Plus, I'm already stretching myself a bit with all the work I'm doing with Dawn."

It'd taken no thought at all to team up with Dawn and offer her own medical skills to the pack. Dawn understood a lot about the human body, and Stephanie knew the ins and outs of animals. They hoped to make some breakthroughs as they put their heads together. It took extra time out of Stephanie's schedule, but she knew it was well worth it.

"That's true." Annie stood from behind the computer, and Jacques padded out from under the desk, lifted his tiny rear into a downward dog stretch and yawned. "We've been booked solid for at least the past month with no end in sight. It's not leaving us room for emergencies."

"I know. That concerns me, and I think we'll need to figure out what times we can block out to allow for that. We'll discuss it in the morning, though. I'm beat. Do you want to come over for dinner tonight? Bennett said he was smoking a pork butt for sandwiches, so I know there'll be plenty." No matter how much her workday had taken out of her, Stephanie was always excited to get home. Bennett was proving to be more of a domesticated wolf than she'd ever imagined, working hard on his cooking skills, and his delicious meals gave her that much more to look forward to.

"No, thanks. I'm actually having dinner with Dad tonight." As Annie reached up to get her jacket off the hook, she looked back at Stephanie and wiggled her shoulders. "I get to meet his new boyfriend."

"Well, that's exciting! How long have they been dating?" Stephanie clipped leashes to each of the dogs.

Annie turned off the lights in the lobby. "I'm not sure. A month? Maybe more? Dad's been pretty secretive about the whole thing because he didn't want to introduce me to someone until he knew there was a chance it was going somewhere. I told him I'm not a little kid and don't mind, but it's a matter of principle for him. Anyway, he's really excited about it. It's adorable."

"Good for him." Stephanie smiled as she, Annie, and the dogs headed out the back door to their vehicles. The dogs loaded up quickly in Stephanie's truck, knowing the routine. "Have fun with your dad tonight."

"I will. Tell Bennett I said hi." Annie hopped in her car and fired up the engine.

Stephanie watched her drive away before she pulled out of her spot. Her little girl had really grown up. She could see it now more than ever. Was her wolf giving her a new glow of life? Stephanie thought she saw it in herself when she looked in the mirror, knowing her beast was thriving inside her.

Rambo came flying out to the garage as soon as she pulled up, jumping and yapping as he greeted her and his new packmates. He scampered back and forth between her truck and the door to the kitchen, so excited he could barely handle himself.

Stephanie could feel his mind without even trying these days, and his elation filled her own body with joy. "Hi, buddy. I'm happy to see you, too." She might understand much of what was going on in their brains, but she couldn't help her old habit of talking to them out loud. From what she could tell, they liked it.

Bennett was standing in the kitchen, shredding a huge pork butt with a pair of plastic claws. He leaned over as she came in, keeping his hands over the cutting board as he kissed her. "Good day?"

"Even better now. It smells absolutely heavenly in here. These guys are enjoying it, too." Sherlock, Penelope, and Jacques all had their noses in the air. Their natural desire for meat was definitely at the forefront of their minds. "Looks like we'll have plenty for a few days."

"It's a good thing, too, because I'll probably be

out all evening tomorrow." Bennett nodded toward the thick file folder on the kitchen table.

"More surveillance work?" Stephanie washed her hands and found the whole wheat buns in the bread basket. She popped a few of them under the broiler to toast.

"Yeah. I was going to ask if you could take Rambo to work with you. He was always used to being here alone when it was just him and me, but now I feel bad if he's waiting here for one of us to return."

"I was actually planning to ask you about that." The dogs were exchanging the various smells they'd picked up during the day. The younger three had all sorts of information about people and animals who'd come into the clinic. Rambo really only had cooking smells or a faint whiff of a rabbit, but he was just as enthused about them. "It might be nice for him to get out a bit."

Bennett tossed the shredded meat with a bit of his homemade sauce in a big bowl. They piled their sandwiches high, topped them with coleslaw, and then added steamed vegetables on the side before they carried their plates to the table.

"How does your new line of work feel so far?" Stephanie asked, poking a finger at the file folder.

Her curiosity made her want to look inside, but this was Bennett's business. She wouldn't interfere.

He chewed thoughtfully. "You know, it's a lot better than I thought it'd be. I was worried I'd only be taking photos of people's spouses cheating on them, but it hasn't really been like that at all. I helped a woman track down her birth parents so she could finally meet them. I've also had a few attorneys contact me about gathering evidence for court cases. Not as heartwarming, but easy enough. Oh, and I've got a guy who wants me to help him with his family tree."

Stephanie nearly choked on her pulled pork. "Seriously? That's a surprise."

"It was to me, too, but then I realized how much sense it made. I'm used to sifting through facts, finding the truth, and checking public records. Who better than a former detective to help someone sort out who's who in their ancestry?" Bennett polished off his sandwich.

"I'm glad you've found something that's working out so well for you." Though Stephanie hadn't been thrilled with the idea of what he did for a living when they'd finally found each other again, she'd never try to talk him out of it. Bennett, however, had wanted to make a change that would be better for their future and keep them safer. He'd even taken down a few of the security devices around his place, but he'd left most of them around for good measure.

"I have, but my favorite part is when I'm off work." After rinsing his plate, he came around behind her chair and took her empty one. "I thought I'd see if you wanted to go for a run tonight."

She grinned up at him. "You read my mind. I thought I was the one who was supposed to do that."

"It's only fair that I get a chance every once in a while."

They stepped out the back door with the dogs right on their heels. Stephanie had already had a bit of a lesson in how to do this before Bennett had marked her, but it was nothing compared to the actual experience. She'd been pleased to find that after a few iterations, she had it down. She steadied her breath and called up her inner wolf. It was right there below the surface, just as it always was, waiting and ready. With an exhale, she let it out. Her fingers shortened into paws with thick nails extending from the ends. Her hearing and sense of smell improved dramatically as her skull reconfigured to allow for this form. The deep stretch of her spine had hurt the first few times, but now it was better than a good massage.

Where do you want to go tonight? Bennett's voice was in her mind as he appeared at her side, his massive gray body just as appealing as his human one. *I cleared out some old tripwires on a trail to the west that you haven't had a chance to see yet.*

Sounds good to me. Hang on. As Stephanie and Bennett had started loping across the backyard, Sherlock was heading south. His nose was to the ground, his mind thrilled with the possibility of what he might find.

Though they didn't speak the same language and she couldn't truly communicate with them any better than she could with her patients at the clinic, Stephanie had learned these dogs well enough that she could interpret their thoughts into close approximations of what their dialog would be if they were capable of the English language.

There's something out there. Sherlock's nose covered swaths of ground as he slowly moved forward, absorbing all the information his sharp nose could pick up. *It could be that rabbit that got away from us last night.*

Jacques raced to his side. He didn't have the sense of smell that Sherlock did, so he bounced up and down and yapped instead. *I'll tear him to pieces this time!*

Me, too! Rambo had been lingering behind them, but the sudden excitement had finally caught his interest.

Penelope looked helplessly back and forth between the dogs heading south and the two wolves, worrying equally about both. *I can't let any of them go off on their own like that!* She whined, unable to decide.

Stephanie nudged Bennett's shoulder. *They're desperate to head south again.*

Like having a bunch of kids, Bennett said with a laugh. *Guess we'd better go, then!*

The two wolves and four dogs took off. Sherlock headed up the pack, guiding the way with his nose. The little dogs served as guards, or at least they thought they did. Penelope watched them all carefully. Stephanie and Bennett brought up the back, trotting along the trail a little slower and taking their time.

Every now and then, Stephanie caught glimpses of the full moon. She had learned so much about these creatures that she'd never known existed, a creature she'd now become herself. There was still so much more, and it intrigued her. It wasn't just the biological and scientific. It was the mystical, the magical, the unknown. She had her whole life to discover more, and she'd get to do it with Bennett right by her side.

THE END

If you enjoyed Bennett and Stephanie's story, read on for a preview of Hayden and Jessica's story, *Firefighter Midlife Wolf*!

HAYDEN

"Turn left in three hundred feet."

"Yeah, turn left. Right into the next disaster," Jessica Anderson grumbled as she looked for the next street sign and did as the GPS told her. She thought she knew her way around Eugene until she'd had to drive all over town. Going to the grocery store or the farmers' market was one thing. Finding the homes of her new patients was a different story, yet it seemed to be the least challenging part of this new job.

Jessica turned into the small parking lot of the senior living apartments. She parked the car before grabbing her tablet and double-checking that she'd entered the correct address for Verna Muldoon. She'd already transposed someone's house numbers once, confusing everyone about why a visiting nurse had shown up at the door. If she was lucky, no one would call her agency and complain. That was the last thing she needed on her first day.

Getting out, Jessica stepped around the car and grabbed her nursing bag from the passenger seat. After the handle had gotten caught on the shifter and half the contents had spilled out earlier that morning, she'd decided it was much easier to just go around. There was no doubt she was learning a lot, but this was making her feel incompetent as hell. Why didn't she just stay where she knew what she was doing? Where she didn't have to question where things were? At the ER, she was on her own turf. She was the one in charge. She should just go crawling back to the admin nurse and ask for her job back.

And have to deal with Brandon again?

It was her wolf more than her human reminding her of exactly why it'd been time to find a new job. No one wanted to work alongside their ex-husband. That arrogant, self-centered jerk was a constant reminder of her failed marriage, especially with that condescending tone. He never would've quit the ER, and so it was up to her. She'd already proven she was strong enough to leave him. Now, she just had to prove she was strong enough to handle this new position.

Stepping up onto the small porch, she spotted the lockbox on the handle and pulled her tablet out again. It felt so awkward to just walk right into a stranger's home. Yes, she had the code, so she had permission, but that didn't really make it any better. Jessica continued the pep talk she'd been giving herself all day, remembering all the awkward things she'd had to do throughout nursing school and as she'd gotten established with her career. No matter how much passion she'd had for helping people, it'd still taken time to not feel weird about touching people's bodies and performing procedures that made them uncomfortable.

She punched the code into the lockbox and hit the unlock button. It beeped loudly at her three times, but she didn't hear the whirring sound of the lock opening. She tried the handle just to be sure. Nope. Still locked. Jessica entered the code again but got three loud beeps once more. "Ugh, come on," she groaned. As she touched the numbers for the third time, she thought for sure this would be both her first and last day of work as a visiting nurse. Instead, the lock opened.

If that was the worst thing to happen during this visit, she'd count herself lucky.

No lights were on in the apartment. Only the muted sunshine from the overcast day provided any illumination as it came in through the back sliding door. It showed Jessica that this was one of the higher-end senior living units, with premium flooring, solid wood cabinets, and fine furniture. She blinked as she tried to let her eyes adjust, though she'd much rather turn on a lamp. After a moment, she spotted a gray head poking up over the back of an armchair near the electric fireplace.

"Hi, Verna," she called out in a gentle voice, not wanting to alarm her in case she hadn't heard the door opening. "My name is Jessica Anderson. I'm your nurse today. How are you?"

The chair swiveled around. Verna glared at her with dark, fiery eyes. "Clear yourself!" she barked.

Jessica had been reaching into her bag, ready to check Verna's vitals and do a quick assessment, but paused with her hand halfway inside the zipper. "I'm sorry?"

"As you should be, coming in here without taking precautions. Clear yourself!" The old woman pointed a sharp finger at the door.

Precautions? Oh. Jessica understood. "Would you

like me to take off my shoes? It's not a problem at all." She gestured toward her feet.

Verna slapped her bony hands down on the arms of her chair. "The universe only knows where you've been and what you've picked up out there! I won't have you bringing negative energies into my home. And don't tell me you don't have any because everyone does. Probably have some nasty spirits clinging to you, as well."

This woman was *not* talking about germs. Jessica's eyes had adjusted to the dim light now. She spotted an array of crystals on the mantle among the framed family photos. A small circle of wood carved with a grid pattern sat on the end table, and several candles were arranged carefully on it. A short stick of twisted wood with a stone wired onto the end rested nearby, appearing to be some sort of wand. She was starting to understand.

"I'm so sorry, Verna. Would you mind telling me what I need to do to clear myself? I'm afraid I haven't done it before." So much for a smooth appointment. This day was just getting better and better. She'd angered her patient without even trying.

"You walked right past it when you came in the door." Verna pointed again.

Turning around, Jessica went back the way she'd

come. The side table near the door held a large abalone shell, and a bundle of pale leaves rested inside it.

"Light that sage until it starts to smoke," Verna commanded. "Then pass it all around your body. You can't just *do* it, either. There has to be some intention behind it to clear yourself of anything that no longer serves you."

Maybe I should clear myself of this damn job. Jessica held back a snicker as she slipped her bag off her shoulder to set it down.

"Sage that, too!"

"Okay." She kept her voice light and airy, something she had plenty of practice at even when times were less than ideal. Jessica picked up the box of matches next to the abalone shell and lit one. She held the flame to the sage, moving it around a little. It didn't seem to be doing much, and she was just about to risk her neck by asking Verna for advice when the end of the bundle burst into flames. "Shit!"

"Blow on it, but gently." The old woman was keeping a keen eye on her from her armchair. "You let it burn for too long, but it can't be helped now. Hell, maybe you needed the extra smoke."

Jessica's hand was shaking as she held up the smoking smudge stick. "So I just pass it around me, like this?" She waved the thing back and forth in front of herself.

"All over. Get your bag, too. Behind you. Over your head. You didn't get low enough. Get your feet." She issued orders every two seconds as the thick plume of smoke started to fill the tiny apartment.

"That's probably good, right?" Jessica coughed. The smell was so strong. Her nose wasn't as sensitive as it would be in her wolf form, but it was still far too much. She waved the smoke away from her face, but there was so much that she couldn't really get away from it. And now what the hell was she supposed to do with this thing? Her instinct was to douse it in the kitchen sink, but at this point, she didn't want to do anything without Verna's permission.

Verna narrowed her eyes, and for a moment, Jessica wondered if she was trying to see whether or not any negative energies were still hanging around. "Just press the burning end into the shell and leave it there."

"Um, okay." Jessica did so, but she still didn't like it. "Isn't there something I should do to put it out?"

"It'll go out if you press it down long enough. The shell represents the water element, after all."

A shrill alarm blasted through the living room. Jessica jumped.

"It's that damn smoke detector!" Verna pointed at the ceiling. "Wave the smoke away from it!"

Jogging over to the small device, Jessica flapped her hand at it. It continued its horrendous beeping, and Jessica now realized just how adorable those tiny beeps from the lockbox had been in comparison. "There's too much. I'm going to open the door."

"Ugh! It's too late," Verna shouted over the clamor. "It's going to call the damn fire department on me."

Jessica swung the door open, and the draft pulled a small amount of the smoke outside. She waved the door back and forth on its hinges, trying to create a current that would clear the place. "Do you have a fan I could plug in?"

"Mrs. Muldoon, this is Trevor with MediCheck." The voice boomed through the living room.

Great. The emergency response system. It was a good thing to have when it was necessary, but Jessica really didn't need any more witnesses to her embarrassing predicament. Verna was more than enough. The day was now picking up speed as it continued to career downhill. At least she could tell them it was just a bit of smoke and everything was fine.

"Is everything okay?" Trevor asked from the speaker on the table.

"It's fine!" Verna's eyes shot daggers at the speaker. "I didn't need this stupid system anyway."

"Mrs. Muldoon, I've got a report of smoke in your home. Are you all right?" Trevor tried again.

"I said I'm fine!" she shouted.

"The fire department is on the way," Trevor announced.

Well, this was it. Her whole career was going straight down the toilet in just one day. "I think you have to push the button for him to hear you." She pointed at the little plastic pendant that hung from Verna's neck as she continued with the door. It was helping, but obviously not enough.

"Oh, this damn thing!" Verna fumbled with the pendant. "It's no use. They'll be here in about two seconds anyway. They always are."

The wail of sirens came through the room as Jessica continued flailing the door back and forth. "Maybe you can call them again and tell them it's a mistake."

If Verna heard her, she made no move to follow her advice. "Damn doctor insisted that I put the thing in, but I don't need it. If I set fire to the place, I'll just call those assholes myself!"

The sirens were getting louder very quickly. The fire department was just down the street from the

senior living complex, and a giant red fire engine
glided into place just in front of Verna's door.

Great. Just fucking great. Jessica stepped aside and
slid open a window as two firefighters stepped over
the threshold.

"Is everyone okay?"

"I'm sorry," Jessica said as she pulled the curtain
to the side to make sure it didn't get in the way of any
airflow. "Everything is fine. We tried to tell the
dispatcher."

The first one had broad shoulders and deep blue
eyes. He lifted his chin slightly as he sniffed the air,
then cocked his head at Verna and put his fists on
his hips. "Mrs. Muldoon, were you burning sage
again?"

Verna scowled at him. "I'll do what I want in my
home, young man!"

"I'm so sorry," Jessica repeated. "This was all my
fault. I didn't know what I was doing." She stopped
short of continuing her explanation as she turned to
look fully at the man who'd spoken. Did she know
him from somewhere?

The other burly firefighter's blue eyes twinkled
just the same. "You really ought to have people
watch a tutorial or something."

"Why would I do that when I can get two hunks

in my apartment with just a bit of smoke?" Verna snarked. "Don't you two have a calendar to pose for or something? It's not like you ever do any real work around here."

The first man pressed his lips together in an attempt to hold back a laugh. "I'll get the fans."

Jessica's mouth gaped as she understood this wasn't the first time this had happened. In fact, the firefighters hadn't even come in their full gear. They wore thick, heavy pants and boots, but the jackets and helmets had been left on the engine with the water hose. They'd known as soon as they'd gotten the call that there was no real emergency.

The first firefighter saw Jessica gawking. He turned and held out his hand. "You must be Verna's latest victim. I'm Hayden, and this is my brother Pierce. It's nice to meet you."

"Jessica Anderson." As she took his big, rough hand, Jessica realized she didn't know this man at all. But her wolf certainly did.

———

ALSO BY MEG RIPLEY
ALL AVAILABLE ON AMAZON

Shifter Nation Universe

Mates Under the Mistletoe: A Shifter Nation Christmas Collection

Marked Over Forty Series

Fated Over Forty Series

Wild Frontier Shifters Series

Special Ops Shifters: L.A. Force Series

Special Ops Shifters: Dallas Force Series

Special Ops Shifters Series (original D.C. Force)

Werebears of Acadia Series

Werebears of the Everglades Series

Werebears of Glacier Bay Series

Werebears of Big Bend Series

Dragons of Charok Universe

Daddy Dragon Guardians Series

Shifters Between Worlds Series

Dragon Mates: The Complete Dragons of Charok Universe

Collection (Includes Daddy Dragon Guardians and Shifters Between Worlds)

More Shifter Romance Series

Beverly Hills Dragons Series

Dragons of Sin City Series

Dragons of the Darkblood Secret Society Series

Packs of the Pacific Northwest Series

Compilations

Forever Fated Mates Collection

Shifter Daddies Collection

Early Novellas

Mated By The Dragon Boss

Claimed By The Werebears of Green Tree

Bearer of Secrets

Rogue Wolf

ABOUT THE AUTHOR

Steamy shifter romance author Meg Ripley is a Seattle native who's relocated to New England. She can often be found whipping up her next tale curled up in a local coffee house with a cappuccino and her laptop.

Download *Alpha's Midlife Baby,* the steamy prequel to Meg's Fated Over Forty series, when you sign up for the Meg Ripley Insiders newsletter!

Sign up by visiting www.authormegripley.com

<u>Connect with Meg</u>

amazon.com/Meg-Ripley/e/B00Z8I9AXW
tiktok.com/@authormegripley
facebook.com/authormegripley
instagram.com/megripleybooks
bookbub.com/authors/meg-ripley
goodreads.com/megripley
pinterest.com/authormegripley

Printed in Great Britain
by Amazon